The BLUELINER

A Chesterboro University Novel

JOSIE BLAKE

For Jessica. You're the bestest bestie a girl could have.

For my hockey family (you know who you are). I'm lucky to share this all with you.

And for my three guys... I love you most.

Blueliner

(noun) - a defenseman in ice hockey

Shea

"HE GOT ENGAGED." MELANIE Peterson squeezes my hand. Her smile is equal parts sympathy and pity. "Last week."

"Engaged." I tilt my head, and my nose wrinkles like she's speaking another language as a rushing sound fills my head. "Justin?" I need clarification. "He got engaged?"

Because her son, Justin Peterson, my ex-boyfriend, said four months ago that he wasn't ready for a commitment. He said he needed space and that he was going off to law school, it was a huge change, and he had to focus on his career right now.

When he said he wasn't ready to commit, I guess he only meant he wasn't ready to commit to *me*.

Around me, the conversation continues. This annual party is one of the dozen or so times a year when my family is all under the same roof. Since my brother got drafted and signed a contract to play hockey for the Philadelphia Tyrants, my mom has thrown this yearly end-of-the-summer party. It might even have started before that. I can't remember. But it's always right before I go back to school and he goes to training camp.

I've never attended this picnic without Justin as my date. Today, I wore a new dress in a color I love, a pretty pink-to-peach gradient, and held my head up. Justin always said I should wear

Contents

Content edits provided by Jessica Ruddick.

Line editing suggestions provided by Red Adept Editing.

ISBN: 978-1-955887-01-4

brighter colors, that they look better on me. It feels good to ignore his voice in my head.

Melanie takes a healthy drink of her champagne. "He met Isabella on his summer internship in San Diego. She's from Colombia."

"Columbia in South Carolina?" I don't know what else to say. "Or in Missouri?"

"The country. In South America."

"Oh." *Don't they speak Spanish in Colombia? Justin doesn't know Spanish.* I force the muscles in my face to make a smile. "Well, that's... wonderful."

"Yes," my mother pipes in, patting my arm. Her voice is too peppy. "It is. We're so happy for him."

Melanie glances between us like we're insane, but she's too sophisticated to say so. "Thank you. It's very sudden."

Sudden? Definitely sudden—like a car wreck. I smile wider, and my grin feels more solid. My mother was a Southern debutante. I know how to remain composed. "Congratulations to you and Rick. That's really exciting news."

She visibly winces. "Thank you, dear. We always expected..." She shrugs, but it's truly apologetic, and I remember again how much I like her and her husband. "Well, anyway. I wanted to let you know before he arrived." She sips her drink again. "You deserve at least that."

I hug her. "I really appreciate that."

Melanie and my mother have done charity work together for as long as I remember, both championing the causes of food and housing insecurity throughout New York City and across Long Island. They've been friends for decades, so I'm sure that telling me about Justin's engagement is difficult.

"I wish him only happiness." It's not entirely true. Sometimes I wish him to get a paper cut in the crack of his knuckle that takes weeks to heal. In particularly low times over the past few months, I've been even less charitable. But most of the time, I wonder how I could have been stupid enough to stay with him for so long.

Justin always had an excuse. There was always a reason why he couldn't come to visit me and why I needed to go to him. Eventually, I stopped asking him to travel for me and just assumed I'd be driving the two hours to his college when I wanted to see him.

There were always reasons why he didn't return calls, too—a study group, some project that ran late, an unexpected nap. A get-together that leaving early would make him feel rude. Foolishly, I stopped asking for explanations about that stuff as well.

When I caught him cheating on me the first time, he gave a tearful apology that I should never have accepted. I didn't listen the second time. That was when he started going on and on about commitment and his career. It was also when I figured out that there would always be some reason why he treated me badly and that all of his reasons made perfect sense to him. I told him goodbye at that point.

"If you'll excuse me," I say, patting both my mother and Melanie on the arm while keeping the polite smile plastered on my lips, "I'm going to find Colt. It was nice seeing you, Melanie."

"You, too, honey." She pulls me in for another hug. "I'll see you in October, at the Food Bank Gala."

"Right." My stomach drops. "The gala. In October." *Damn it, I forgot about that.*

My mom wraps her arm around me and squeezes. "It's an annual event. Our entire family attends. Of course she'll be there."

That's not true. For the past two years, while Colt has played for the Tyrants, he's missed it. Lucky duck.

"Right. Of course." I keep smiling like a beauty queen, like my damn facial features are part of a suit of armor. "I'll see you in October. At the gala." I let my face drop after I leave them as I head for the patio. I need some air.

Like the inside rooms, the pool and gardens are full of people, but it's more family-oriented—kids swimming, and people are playing yard games or sitting in the shade. It's humid, and the air out here hits me like a smack in the face... or like the unexpected knowledge that the boy I broke up with less than a season ago is already engaged.

I shake my head, blowing out a breath. When I get to the bar, I grab a flute of champagne and down it in a couple gulps before reaching for another.

"Slow down, lush." My twin brother arrives and lounges against the bar next to me, grinning behind aviator sunglasses. "You know that stuff goes to your head." I scoot down a step to give him more space. A forward for the Philadelphia Tyrant hockey team, he's tall, broad, and in tiptop shape, something he definitely knows. In swim trunks and a polo shirt, he oozes ego. If I didn't know him so well and love him so dearly, I might think he was a cocky ass. Sometimes, I still do.

I roll my eyes at him. "That's not true." It's totally true, but this is my brother. He can't always be right. I toast him with the second one. "Trust me, this is much needed." I take another healthy sip. "You should have one too."

"Yeah?" He asks, reaching for a flute. "I wasn't planning on drinking today. Need to run in the morning." Training camp doesn't start for a couple weeks, but he's only been on the team for two years. He still feels a lot of pressure to prove himself. Or he's just a workaholic. Either way, he takes his workout regimen and carb consumption seriously.

"Justin got engaged."

He gags on a sip of champagne. Sputtering, he erupts into a fit of coughing. I take the opportunity to finish my second drink. "What?" he finally asks.

"Last week. Melanie told me." I signal to the bartender. "You want something stronger?"

"No." He shakes his head, wiping the corner of his mouth. "That pansy-ass, whiny, sniveling, crybaby dickhead." He sets his flute down with enough force that the people next to us glance at him. "I never liked that guy, Shea."

"I know." He isn't the only one. Most of my friends from high school and my college friends who had met him... no one liked him. To be fair, Justin never made any real attempts with any of them. Now that I've had a few months away from him, I don't think it was because he didn't like them. More likely, he didn't think they were worth his time. I should have recognized what a huge red flag that was.

I sigh. "He wasn't all bad." But I need to remind myself too. He'd been fun to be with, charismatic. Especially in the beginning. Much like Colt, people congregated around him. It was easy to get swept up in being with someone like that. It's easy to mistake arrogance for confidence.

"I don't care if he saves puppies and helps little old ladies across the street. He was an asshole to you"—he leans in and enunciates— "a *disloyal* asshole." To Colt, that's the greatest insult. My brother isn't perfect, but he's protective of those he cares about.

"Yeah."

"Is he coming?" His eyes stray to the door. "Is that why Melanie told you?"

"Yeah."

"Shit." His face wrinkles in distaste.

That about covers it. "I can do this." I pick up another champagne flute and sip.

Colt gives me the side-eye and retrieves it from my fingers.

"It's been three months, and I've learned a lot." As in, I've wondered repeatedly what I'd been doing with him. "I'm going to be a senior at Chesterboro, and I haven't been single since high school. This year, I'm going to focus on that. On me." It's the first time I've said it, but it's the right thing for me. "I don't want a boyfriend right now."

"I'm on board with all that." He toasts me with my own flute.

The alcohol is definitely working. I sway on my feet, and Colt takes another drink from my glass. "Hey, that's mine." I swipe it back from him. "I'm twenty-one. Most girls I know have already slept with lots of other guys." I wave my arms, forgetting that I'm holding my champagne, which sloshes over the side.

Colt leans closer and whispers, "You should say that louder. Mr. and Mrs. Shumacher at the end of the bar didn't hear you."

Eyes wide, I cover my mouth with my hand and put the glass down. He's right. That's probably enough champagne for now.

He shifts closer, his brows furrowed. "Is that what you want? To sleep with random guys?"

"Yes. No." I don't know what I want. I huff, frustrated. "I was with Justin for a long time. And he's the only…"

My twin closes his eyes, shaking his head and waving his hand at me.

Right, he doesn't want to hear about my love life. Not that it was much to write home about. I start again. "I wasted four years with him."

"Waste..." He shrugs. "Maybe. But I never saw you as a casual fling kind of girl."

"What does that mean?" I glare at him, hands on my hips. "That's not true." I was a girlfriend for years. It wasn't that great.

"It is true"—he chuckles— "in the best kind of way. You take care of people. You get involved. You fix things. Hell, if not for you, a slacker like Justin Peterson would never have gotten into law school."

"That's also not true." Justin had the right skill set for law school—easygoing charisma, an ability to debate, to bullshit. He only needed some encouragement and someone to believe in him.

"Whatever. I'm only saying to be careful, Tiny."

I wince at the nickname Colt and his best friend, Linc, had given me back in grade school. Even then, I was small. I'm barely average height at five-three, but I'm petite. They've always been tall, long-limbed, and rangy, even then. Now, they're both well over six feet and walls of muscle. I'm always the shrimp.

"Where is Linc, anyway? He usually comes to this." If he skips, it won't surprise me. I haven't seen him since we got home from school in May. Usually, he spends as much time with Colt as he can. They're practically brothers. But this year, they've only gotten together a couple times that I know of and always somewhere else. Colt said he's been working a lot, but that sounds like an excuse.

"He said he'd be here soon. He was working a project with his dad today." A wrinkle appears between his brows. "Have you noticed he hasn't been around much?"

"Yeah. Did you do something wrong?"

He scowls at me. "Why would it be me?"

"You're the best friend."

"Well, you go to school with him."

I sigh. "I don't know. I invited him to hang out when Violet and Nate were in town, but he was working then too." He was probably better off missing that. Vi and Nate had been dating almost a year, but they definitely didn't look happy when I saw them.

"Maybe business is really busy." Linc helps his father with their family construction business when he's home from school.

"Maybe." But Colt doesn't look convinced either. His gaze strays over my shoulder, and his face clouds. "We'll have to see what's up with him. But first, let's get through this." He nudges his head toward the door.

There, under the awning, is my ex-boyfriend and a tall, gorgeous girl with huge boobs. She's got long dark hair and olive skin that's glowing in a sundress that's barely covering her butt. She looks like a model. I'm not sure what I expected, but she isn't it.

I stand up straight and square my shoulders. "I'm going to go say hello."

"Do you think that's smart?" He glances at me. "You're, well, tipsy."

"No, I'm not." *I completely am.* "Fine, you're right, but what else can I do? This isn't going to get any easier if I put it off."

Our mothers already mentioned the gala. We're going to see each other.

"Come on, then." Colt offers me his arm. "At least hang on to me. Why do you always have to wear those heels?"

I glance down at the three-inch sandals on my feet. "You're the one who calls me Tiny. I'm short." That's not entirely true. I'm pretty average, just short next to him.

He shakes his head. "Right."

Together, we head across the pool deck and toward them.

One moment, I'm clinging to Colt's arm. We move around a couple and their two children. The younger one is about two, and he's wearing floaties and pulling against his mother. He screams at the top of his lungs about how he wants to go back in the water.

He slips her grip and falls back into me. I stumble. It could be the heels, or maybe it's the champagne, but I'm certainly on the edge of the pool, where the lip is slippery concrete, not the patio bricks from everywhere else. I lose my footing then fall, hitting the cool pool water with a splash before going under.

Linc

I FINISH OFF THE water jug I bought at the convenience store this morning then wipe the sweat off my forehead, sure I'm leaving a layer of dirt there. I wish I'd bought two gallons of water. The summer heat hasn't let up even at six o'clock.

"Good work today. That was a long one." My father packs his tools beside me. We stayed late at this construction site because there was some detailed woodworking that needed to be finished, and neither of us wanted to quit before it was done. "You've been a huge help this summer."

It's high praise from my dad. A man of few words, he doesn't dole out empty compliments. My throat tightens up. "Thanks for having me, Dad."

He snorts softly. "Right." He doesn't say it, but we both know that I'm the one who did him the favor. The past couple years, I wasn't around much during the summer, spending the time with hockey trainers or at camps. This year is different for lots of reasons that he and I don't talk much about.

When I'm not here, he hires someone to help him out on his jobs, which cuts into his take-home pay. I'm the oldest of four, and my mother had to quit teaching full time, thanks to the physical toll of MS. She tutors and works part time at the community college, but it's not the same as full-time work with benefits.

"You skate today?" he asks.

I lower the jug and look at him. I guess we are going to talk about why things are different these days.

"No." Some panic and sweating in the parking lot but no skating. "I went to the gym, though. Got in a good workout." I replace the cap on my water then tuck it into my bag so I can recycle it later.

"I'm sure you did." My father sorts his tools, making sure he's got everything, same as every day at the end of the job. He's meticulous with them, slow and steady, like he is with everything. "Not the ice, though."

That's as close as my dad will ever get to telling me that I'm screwing something up. His concern weighs on me, adding to the shame I'm already carrying around. A wave of anger follows on the heels of that hit of guilt, and I swallow it all down. This is my dad. Besides, he's not the one I'm pissed at. I see that guy in the mirror every day.

I don't know what my deal is either. The doctor cleared me to skate in the spring. After sitting on the bench all season last year with concussions, I'm physically ready to get back out there. This is my year to shine. I'm a senior, and it's the last year I have to convince the team that drafted me, the Boston Gladiators, to sign me to a contract to play in the NHL.

I might be physically ready, but my head sure isn't in it.

"You going to the rink tonight?"

"No," I grumble, sliding into the passenger seat. I turn the truck on so the air conditioning can get going. "I got this, Dad."

"Doesn't look like it." He climbs behind the steering wheel and buckles up. I mess with the radio, not making eye contact.

"Tonight. I'll go with you." He pats the steering wheel. "We'll go home and grab some showers, and I'll come with you."

"No." It's so quick that he raises his eyebrows at me. "Don't you want to see Mom, check on how she's doing?" It's a low blow. My mother is in the middle of a flare-up, so I'm leaning on his weakness. But getting back on the ice... it's something I need to do, and I don't want him there to see me chicken out again. "Besides, I'm supposed to go to the Carmichaels'. Their annual end-of-summer party."

"Fine. But don't think this distracts me from the skating thing, though," he adds. "You need to stop putting this off and get yourself out there."

"I know, Dad." He's right. The longer I wait to get on the ice, the harder it is. I need to suck it up and stop being a pussy.

I glance at my father as he drives. I lost the money Chesterboro University had given me for room and board this year, thanks to my concussions last year. My tuition is still covered by my scholarships, but I'll need to cover my cost of living off-campus. My father and I have been picking up extra work all summer, trying to get ahead on my rent for the year and save enough that my expenses won't be too much of a hit to my family.

The least I can do is pull my weight. That means making his hard work worth it by going back to school this year and killing it on the rink.

Tomorrow. I need to hit the ice tomorrow.

It's almost seven when I pull my decade-old Nissan to a stop in front of the valet outside the Carmichaels' house. A Rolls, a

Benz, and a Maserati are all parked on the circular drive. My car doesn't fit in here, and the valet wrinkles his nose at it.

The guy probably lives in Hampton Bays like me. I toss him the keys and wink at him. "Take good care of my baby. I don't want any scratches on it."

He snorts, and I chuckle as I bound up the front stairs. At the door, a server offers me an appetizer, and I take one then pop it in my mouth. It's something with bacon, and I snag a second. Mrs. C's food choices are always excellent. Inside, another server offers me champagne, and I pass. Not my thing.

Like all the Carmichael parties, this one is full of influential people. I can almost smell the money from the door. They're all dressed expensively and wear self-importance like part of their outfits.

Coming here is like stepping into another world. My family had a barbecue at my parents' house last weekend. The differences are striking. Here, it's waiters and dainty butler-served appetizers. It's champagne and expensive cocktails made with the best spirits. Somewhere, I bet Mr. Carmichael is holed up with a bunch of his cronies, drinking expensive bourbon and smoking the finest cigars. My family sat at picnic tables over dips and chips and drank sodas and beers, and my father manned the grill while wearing an apron that said, "This guy rubs his own meat."

Mrs. Carmichael sees me from across the room. I'm six-four. I stand out. She waves, and I make my way toward her. It's not hard for me to weave through a crowd. At my height, people tend to move out of my way.

When I get to her side, she opens her arms. Laughing, I lean down so she can hug me and kiss my cheek. While Mr. Carmichael and Colt are both well over six feet, the female

Carmichaels are petite—both only five-three or so. They try to make up for it by wearing high heels, but even then, they're almost a foot shorter than me.

I adore all four of them. They're a second family to me.

"You made it," she says, squeezing my hand before she scowls. "We've barely seen you this summer," she chides.

I rub the back of my neck. She's right—I haven't been around much.

As quickly as the disapproval darkens her features, it's gone, and she smiles at the couple she is speaking with. "Ron, Tina, this is my son's oldest and closest friend, Lincoln Reynolds. They played hockey together as boys. He attends Chesterboro with Shea." She glances at me. "Linc, this is Congressman Ron Gerheart and his wife, Tina."

"Nice to meet you, young man," the congressman says.

"Same to you, sir." I shake their hands, and they smile and make small talk, like we're all the same kind of people. Except that isn't true. They're high-powered politicians, and I'm a kid from Hampton Bays who can barely find rent money for college this year.

After an appropriate amount of time and small talk, Mrs. Carmichael squeezes my arm. "The kids are outside by the pool. Why don't you join them?"

"Thank you. If you'll excuse me," I nod at the Gerhearts. "It was nice to meet you both."

"You too." I step away, but not before I overhear Congressman Gerheart comment, "What a polite young man. Did he go to Prep with your kids?"

I almost laugh. My parents couldn't have afforded the down payment at Prep. I head out the side door and scan the scene for the Carmichael twins. It doesn't take long to find them.

Separately, they're two of the most striking people I've ever met, but together, they're the kind of arresting that makes me pause. Colt is tall and broad like I am, if not an inch or two shorter, which still makes him taller than most of the people around. According to the attention he's gotten from girls all these years, he's pretty good-looking. Now, with his shaggy dark hair and tan, there are more than a few women—single and otherwise—checking him out.

But it's his sister, Shea, who steals my breath. That's not surprising, really. She's been doing it since she was in middle school.

This evening, she's wearing some peachy-pink dress with thin straps at the shoulder. It hits her mid-thigh, and it's nothing special, but she's this petite thing with legs that go on for miles. Tonight, those legs are accentuated with strappy brown sandals.

The siblings have similar coloring, but Shea's skin glows. Her hair isn't only dark, like Colt's, it's a whole bunch of shades of brown, from dark coffee to warm caramel. It's thick, wavy, and long, but today, she's got it piled on top of her head in one of those makeshift buns that probably took a long time to arrange—at least they always take my sisters a long time to get them to look like that. Still, she looks chic and casual. She's gorgeous.

I'm glad they don't see me coming out the side door. It gives me a moment to get my thoughts together. Mrs. Carmichael isn't wrong—I've been avoiding them.

Colt always asks me if I'm back on the ice, and I've run out of excuses for why I'm not. The past couple of weeks, I've been driving to the ice rink where I learned to skate, the one I've been skating at since I was a toddler. Once, I didn't even make it out of my car. I sat there in the parking lot with my heart racing and my palms sweating. The times I do go inside, I lace up and sit on the bench, never taking the ice.

I'm a wimp.

I haven't told him because I can't bring myself to tell him that a few concussions have turned me into a panic-attack-riddled idiot. I've been avoiding him instead, because that's really mature.

And Shea broke up with Justin, and I can't watch her mourn that asshole. Neither Colt nor I liked the guy. He's one of those preppy douchebags who leans hard on his parents' influence. He never deserved her. In my mind, no one will ever be good enough for Shea. Especially me. Because even though she's single, that doesn't mean I ever stand a chance with her. Even if I did, she's my best friend's sister. Strictly off-limits.

I take a deep breath, steadying myself on that certainty, and start toward them.

Everything happens fast after that. A kid gets away from his mother and stumbles backward into Shea, who loses her footing. She slips and falls, crashing into the pool with a splash.

I move without thinking, heading to the edge to see if she's all right. That's when I see her ex-boyfriend.

It's been a while. This past year, he didn't even bother to come to Chesterboro to visit her, the dick. I'd held my tongue, though. Any time I badmouthed the guy—and he gave me plenty of reasons—she'd defend him, and hearing her do that was worse than keeping quiet about how much I didn't like him.

He's all the things a preppy rich boy should be—fresh haircut, collared shirt, clean-shaven. I absently rub my own stubble. No time after work today to shave properly, so I hadn't bothered.

Even though Justin is well-groomed, he's still a slimeball.

Shea comes up sputtering. She pushes her hair out of her face and starts toward the pool stairs. That's when I notice the dress. Wet, it's practically see-through. Through it, I can clearly see the silhouette of her perfect breasts, and I'm hard immediately.

Except everyone else can see her too. I look toward Colt. He meets my eyes, but he's all horrified paralysis. No help at all.

I don't think. I reach for the hem of my shirt and pull it over my head. I have the good sense to empty my pockets—cell phones are expensive—and then I take a running leap toward the edge of the pool. "Cannonball!"

I hit the water perfectly, showering Shea with a spray, and she covers her face, swiping the water away. It's been a year or so, but I've been in the Carmichael pool so many times, I know exactly how deep it is where I land.

There's laughing then another splash and another. Suddenly, the pool is a lot fuller.

"Shea, your dress," I hiss. Her eyes widen, and she glances down. I see the realization that she's practically naked hit her face. A soft-pink flush covers her cheeks. I was hard before, but it's painful now. "Let's get you out of here."

I shuffle her up the stairs, her arms folded over her chest. Colt finally got his head out of his ass, and he's there with a towel, waiting to wrap her in it. We circle around her like the Secret Service or something.

"Are you okay?" I ask. "You didn't twist your ankle or anything?"

Wringing out the water in her hair, she stares up at me. "You came."

What? I scowl. "Of course. I told you guys I'd be here, didn't I?" I haven't been around a lot, but still...

She and Colt exchange their "twin glance," the one that says more than any words.

I sigh. "I wouldn't miss your mother's party."

"But you'll ghost us?" Colt lifts his eyebrow.

He's right. I shrug. "Sorry, man. It's been a rough summer." That doesn't cover it, but I'm not one to whine about my bullshit.

"Well, I've missed you." He leans in to hug me, smacking me on the back. I'm soaked and half-naked, but Colt doesn't care. I clap his back, laughing.

"Come on." I shove him back. "Mind if I borrow some clothes? These got wet." I motion to my khaki shorts. He laughs.

"What's mine is yours, you dick," he says.

I roll my eyes. "Come on, Shea. Let's go get cleaned up." I wink at her and offer my elbow. I haven't seen her in weeks. Now that she's here, it's like something heavy has lifted off my chest.

"No." She holds the towel tighter around her, shaking her head. "I need to say hello to Justin."

"What? Why? You don't owe that guy anything." I look to Colt for support. "Back me up."

He glances between Shea and me then over my shoulder, where I assume Shea's piece-of-shit ex is standing. "He has a point, Shea."

"I don't need permission from either of you." She scowls at us then smooths her hair again, twisting out the edges. Suddenly, her face changes, breaking into a fake smile. "Justin. How are you?"

"Shea."

His voice sets me on edge, so I close my eyes and breathe deep before I turn to face him.

"Good to see you."

He's exactly as I remember him. A few inches shorter than me and as douchey as ever. His hair is cut short, and it's got some sort of product or something in it. Shiny. He's perfectly pressed and smells like expensive cologne. But he's not smiling. Instead, he's glancing between Shea and me, a scowl on his face. "How long have you two been a couple?"

I look around. There's no one here but Shea, Colt, and me. My brain must have shorted out from Shea's see-through clothes because it takes me too long to figure out what the hell he's talking about. "Who, Shea and me?" I take a step away from her.

Justin doesn't respond, only folds his arms over his chest. The girl he came with stands behind him, awkwardly watching the proceedings.

"You're crazy, man." Colt laughs, shaking his head in disbelief. "Linc's known Shea since we were kids. She's practically another sister to him."

Everything in me winces, but I hold myself impassive. I've got almost a decade of practice pretending that's true.

"Please." Justin snorts. "I'm not blind. I'm surprised they waited this long." He pauses. "Maybe you didn't..."

Shea's face whitens. *Because of the insinuation that she's dating me or because he's accusing her of cheating on him?*

Neither is good. I step closer to him, my fists clenched. "You are way off base," I growl at him. "There would never be anything between Shea and me." Not only is she completely out of my league, but Shea's my best friend's sister—forbidden.

Justin opens his mouth, but Shea steps between us, her face still pale. "He's right." She holds the towel against her like it's armor, but her chin is up as she glares at Justin. "We aren't together. Not that it's any of your business. Now if you'll excuse me, I'm going to get changed." She heads toward the house without a backward glance.

Justin gives me another disgruntled snort before he throws his arm over his date's shoulder and they slink away, leaving me with Colt.

"Colt... he's got it wrong..." My skin's too tight. I've been so careful, all these years. I keep everything I've ever thought about Shea on lockdown. That Justin, of all people, might have noticed it... it's loosened the earth under me.

"Please, man." He grips my shoulder, smiling. "He's lost his mind. You're my best friend. You'd never get with my sister. Go get something dry out of my room. I'll smooth things over here."

Shea

MY PARENTS' HAMPTONS HOUSE is on the peninsula. There's a system of porches, patios, and decks that wrap around the entire structure. Every side of the house has a stunning view, something my mother insisted on when it was built. I love the views, sure, but I also love that in the middle of a party that will probably go most of the night, I can still manage to find a quiet place away from everyone else.

This deck is off my father's office. He's downstairs in the den in a cloud of cigar smoke, so the windows behind me are dark.

I pick up the champagne I swiped from the kitchen and take another swig right from the bottle. My mom is right—this stuff *is* good.

My sketchbook rests in my lap, open to a design for an addition to an old Shaker-style home that's scheduled to be renovated. The house has an open garden space in the backyard between two former additions. I'm proposing incorporating the two existing buildings into one larger house, pulling in the garden and creating a space that will complement the structure and remain true to its original architectural integrity. It's probably going to require approval from the historical society, but I've been careful to follow the local historic-preservation guidelines.

My internship this summer was for a company specializing in historically accurate renovations and additions. I loved the whole process—studying the architectural time periods, determining original structures, working to reclaim what had been lost to time and negligence. I'll be back in school in a few days and won't be able to oversee or watch the progress on the Shaker house, but this design has been twisting in my brain all week. I plan to send it to Jackie, my summer boss, as a final piece. I'm going to miss the work.

I stare out over the water, where the moon is full and high in the sky.

After my accidental dunking, I retreated to my room. After seeing the extent of my see-through dress after its journey into the pool, the adrenaline I'd worked up to see Justin seeped away. I got changed, but it took an hour before I had enough courage to go back downstairs, and even then, I texted Colt to make sure that Justin had gone. I mingled a little while, but that was about all I could manage before I bailed.

I'm not proud. Sometimes the best thing to do is to cover losses and try again another day.

"I wondered if I'd find you out here."

Linc. I sigh. I should have expected him. He's a worrier. "Where is Colt?" I'm surprised that they strayed too far from each other. Usually, when they're together, it's hard to separate them.

"Patricia? Alyssa?" He shakes his head. "Something like that. She caught him by the dessert table, and he hasn't been able to get away."

"Tricia." I laugh. Tricia MacFarland has been following my brother's career since he was a kid. She's a huge hockey fan and knows more about the stats of different teams than anyone else I know. Her kids are in college, so she has lots of time on her hands. I'm sure she's giving Colt a rundown on the different teams she expects to advance this year.

"I wanted to check on you." He plops down next to me on the bench.

I scoot over, giving him more space. As always, Linc makes everything smaller. "I'm fine. Just wanted some time to myself." More like I needed to hide. I close my eyes, but the events play out there, ringing in my ears.

"How long have you two been a couple?"

"There would never be anything between Shea and me."

Linc is right—Justin is way off base. There's nothing between Linc and me except for the humiliating memory of a thirteen-year-old girl's crush.

In middle school, Colt's other friends either ignored me or picked on me. It was tough, because Colt's more outgoing than I am, and I'm definitely more sensitive. It was hard not to feel like I was always tagging along. But Linc never treated me like a pest, probably because he has so many younger sisters. He's used to having girls around. He always listened to me. Still does.

Not only is he kind, but he's also always been tall and athletic, and he has the most adorable dimple. It made sense that preteen me would swoon over him... until the night I overheard him and Colt talking about me.

Linc had been sleeping over before one of their hockey tournaments. They had a game early the next morning. I hadn't been eavesdropping, at least not intentionally. I was going to wish them good luck because I wouldn't be able to see them before they left. Also, because I wanted to see Linc as often as I could. For some reason, I wouldn't be attending that game. I can't even remember why.

Before I could knock on Colt's bedroom door, though, my name stopped me in my tracks.

"Reggie likes Shea. So back me up in the locker room, will you? I need to chat with him." Through the barely open door, I could see Colt tossing a baseball in the air while he lay on his bed. I shifted so I could see Linc, too, lounging in Colt's desk chair.

I remember thinking that Colt was nuts. Reggie was a complete jerk to me. No way could he have liked me, but boys were weird, so I couldn't be sure.

"Sure." Linc massaged his knuckles. "He likes Shea?" His voice was mild, super casual. But I leaned closer, wondering how he felt about that and if it bothered him that someone else liked me.

"Yeah." Colt wrinkled his nose. "I heard him telling Josh. We're teammates, for fuck's sake. That's not something you do." He sat up, waving his arm at Linc. "Like you... you'd never make a move on my sister, you know? Just like I'd never make a move on yours."

"My sisters are babies." His sisters were eight, six, and an infant. I didn't understand what Colt was getting at.

"You know what I mean." Colt flopped back down and continued tossing the ball. "There are rules. You don't date your friend's sisters." He points at Linc. "Especially not your best friend's sister."

Linc was quiet for a long moment, and I held my breath, dying to see what he would say to that. My young, foolishly romantic heart wanted to hear him say he liked me, too, and that Colt was ridiculous. Instead, he ducked his head and said, "You're right. Your sister might as well be my sister."

"Exactly," Colt exclaimed.

I'd stepped away from the door as quietly as I could and hurried back to my room. I cried myself to sleep that night.

That night, I learned that Linc Reynolds, with his adorable dimple and hot body, could be my friend, but he would never see me as anything more than an extra sister.

That's always been fine. It is what it is. But hearing him write me off as completely undesirable—or at least undateable—in front of Justin, who also found me lacking, well... stuff like that hits you in the ego.

I shift, hugging my knees closer to myself. I don't know why I'm awkward right now. Nothing he said is news to me.

"Justin and his date didn't stay long, if it makes you feel any better. Colt must have gotten rid of them before I even got a chance to change." Linc folds his hands in front of him, leaning on his knees. I shift, arranging the seat cushion I'd propped behind me.

"Fiancée."

"What?"

"Not his date. His fiancée," I repeat. The word is sour on my tongue.

"He's engaged." Linc blinks at me, and I can only shrug. His jaw tightens, and he growls as he stands. Pacing back and forth, he clenches and unclenches his fists. "That low... what a... I can't believe he..." These stops and starts continue for a second, and I use my imagination to fill in the words he opts not to say out loud. I'm sure he's not sparing me from the language. I assume he just can't get the words out. "What a scumbag."

I can't really deny that. It's fine if he starts dating someone. I get that. Justin isn't the kind of guy who likes to be alone. But to get engaged so fast was tacky. Then again, I guess it's not really about me. With him, it's never been about me.

"Why the hell would he come here with his fiancée?" He shakes his head and stops, planting a hand on a hip and pointing at me. "You know he never deserved you, right? He didn't deserve ten minutes of your time, let alone four years."

I grin, and he scowls at me.

"I'm serious."

"I know," I say, laughing. "That's why it's funny."

"It's not funny."

"Okay. It's not funny." Still chuckling, I pull my knees against my chest, tucking my sketchbook closer. "You know what is funny? That he thought... that there was something...you know." I wave my hand between him and me. "Between us. I mean, can you imagine?" I keep the smile on my face, but I immediately regret bringing it up. I should have left it alone, except I'm sure I'll feel worse about it if I don't get it out there in the open.

He winces, chewing on his lip. I want to roll my eyes. It should be illegal for a guy to be this good-looking and yet still so adorable. He sits beside me again. "Listen, Shea, about what I said..."

Oh no. I definitely don't want to listen to anything that starts like that. "Please, stop. I get it. I'm like a sister to you." I nudge him with my shoulder and squeeze his hand, doing what I can to alleviate the tension. I *need* things to be normal between us. I don't have many friends at Chesterboro—not good friends—and I'm not about to make things weird with the ones I do have.

"It doesn't matter, anyway. I don't need to see him again until I have to go to that stupid charity gala in October."

He cocks his head. "What charity gala?"

I wave him off. "My mom and his mom do a lot of charity work with a chain of food banks in the city and boroughs. They throw this annual fundraiser every year. Our whole family goes. Well, Colt has skipped the last couple because he's been traveling. But his schedule might be different this year."

"I see." His mouth twists, though, and I'm not sure he does.

"So, I'll need to find some kind of date." I scowl. "Great."

"I can go with you." He doesn't look at me, only stares out at the water in front of us. "If you need a date."

"Please." I grin, because of course he'd offer. He's always there for me when I need him. "That's sweet, but you were pretty adamant that nothing's going on with us. And nothing would make me look more pathetic than forcing you to go with me." I hug my legs closer, tucking my chin behind my knees.

"I didn't mean it to sound like..." He drops his elbows on his knees again, rubbing his palms together. "You could never be pathetic. I was adamant because I needed to explain..." He runs his hands over his face. He's antsy tonight.

"What were you explaining?"

He stands up again, clearly agitated. "That there'd never be anything between us."

Ouch. "Right. That's what you said."

"But not because of you. Jesus, Shea." He waves a hand, motioning to all of me. "I mean, you're gorgeous. By far the prettiest girl I've ever met. And the most caring. And nicest." He's still scowling, but his words curl warmth in my stomach.

He thinks I'm pretty? I didn't know that. I don't know what to say. "Thank you?"

He snorts. "Like you needed me to tell you any of that." He rolls his eyes. "My point is that any guy would be lucky to be with you. But you're Colt's sister." When I only blink at him, he adds. "Off-limits. Anyone who doesn't get that is an idiot." He shakes his head. "I'm your friend, though. I can take you as your friend. So you don't need to be there alone." He glares at me. Definitely looks like a guy who wants to be my date. If this weren't so sad, it might be funny.

"Well, thanks anyway." The last thing I need is to feel guilty about making him get all dressed up for a stuffy party with me. Usually, guys only do that if there's at least a slim chance they might get laid. Still, the wheels start turning in my head... "But there is something you might be able to do for me."

"What?"

I sit up straighter. Of course. Why hadn't I thought of this earlier? "When we get back to Chesterboro, I'm going to need your help."

"Sure. You know I'd help you do anything."

"Great." I smile, setting my sketchbook in front of me, excited. "Because you are going to help me find the perfect date for this gala."

Linc

"NO." THERE HAS TO be a stronger word for how much of a nope this is. Like, *hell* no. Abso-fucking-lutely not. No, but with the fire of a million suns. Something like that.

"What?" Confusion lights her face. After her unscheduled dip in the pool, she changed into tan shorts and some sort of bohemian tank top. It has thin straps at the shoulders. She didn't dry her hair, I guess, because it's pulled into a braid that falls over her right shoulder.

With no makeup and barefoot, she's as lovely as she was in a dress and high heels.

"No, Shea." No way can I be unbiased enough to help her date anyone.

"Linc, come on..." She reaches for me then squeezes my arm, and the contact sends awareness snaking through my whole body. "You know practically everyone on campus, and if you don't know them, someone you know knows them."

That's true. "How does that make me suited to find you a date?"

"Well, I don't know that many people. I'm going to need help. Meeting people." She shrugs. "I've been off campus a lot. It kept me from making a lot of friends."

"Everyone loves you, Shea." She might not be the outgoing twin, but she's so genuine that it's impossible not to like her. "Hell, half the hockey team is in love with you already." Internally, I balk and consider whether I'm going to need to keep the hockey guys' hands off her. It won't surprise me. There's no way that any of them get near her, though. Shea deserves a good guy, someone smart. The guys on the hockey team are more interested in partying and chasing puck bunnies than being good enough for her.

"Please." She rolls her eyes. "The hockey team only puts up with me because I'm your friend. They wouldn't know I existed if it wasn't for you."

It's like she's never looked in a mirror. "I'm no matchmaker."

"I'm not asking for a fairy godmother." She leans forward. "I just would like your help... vetting them."

"Like with a questionnaire?" I stand up and retreat across the patio. I need space. Hell, I need to run away from this conversation and pretend it never happened.

"No." She scowls at me. "But you'll know if they're decent guys."

"No guy is decent." *What does that even mean?* "Trust me. Every guy can be a pig."

"That's not what I mean. I mean, is a guy... I don't know, kind. Or smart. Or funny. Is he a good friend? Stuff like that. The kind of stuff that would make a good date."

"You're only going to one party with him. I don't understand why I'd need to vet some guy for that."

She narrows her eyes. "It's in New York City. He'd be staying with me, at my parents' place. Or we'd stay at the hotel where the gala is. I'll be spending the whole weekend with him." She glances away. "But it's not only for the gala."

"You're looking for a boyfriend?" The words taste like acid on my tongue.

I'd spent the past years learning to accept that she was with Justin. I thought she was happy. I didn't like him, but she seemed to, so that was enough. It's not like I can be with her. I know that. I only needed to know she was happy. Now, though, I don't think I can watch her find someone new. Not yet. I sure as hell am not going to be able to help.

"No. No boyfriends. God, no." Horror whitens her face in the moonlight. "I've spent most of high school and college being a girlfriend. It's exhausting." She shakes her head, waving the idea off. "I'm looking for someone to spend some time with. Someone who's fun. Maybe someone who likes to do some of the things I do. You know, stuff like that."

Her face flushes, and suddenly I know exactly the kind of stuff she's talking about. "You're looking for a fuck buddy."

"Jesus, Linc." Her eyes are wide. "Why do you have to make it sound so sordid?"

"Who says words like 'sordid'?" I fire back.

She throws the tail of her braid over her shoulder. "You made it sound disgusting."

"It's not disgusting if you're doing it right." I know I shouldn't be talking to her like this. She's Colt's sister. But she had a boyfriend for a long time. She shouldn't seem so uncomfortable.

She sniffs, notching up her chin. "I'm only looking for someone to spend time with."

"In bed."

She glares at me. "Maybe. Not that it's your business."

I want to throw up. No, I want to throw something. I turn from her because watching her flush as she thinks about sleeping with some unknown guy—a guy I'm supposed to help her choose—is probably doing things to my facial features that I'd prefer her not to see.

I lean against the deck railing, staring out at the ocean in front of me. The moon is casting a long swath of light across the water, and I try to figure out what the hell I did in my life that signed me up for this kind of torture.

"I'm not asking you to set me up on dates," she offers softly behind me. "I hoped that you'd be around, in case I have questions about anyone." There's a pause. "You know what? It's not a big deal. This is dumb, and I shouldn't have even mentioned it. I had champagne and, well, we all know how that goes to my head." She laughs, but it's her self-conscious laugh, and it makes me close my eyes.

"Of course," I hear myself say. "I'll always be there for you." I straighten, because when the people you care about need you, you man up. Besides, I'd never let her spend time with someone I thought might hurt her. Turning, I paste a smile on my face and cross my arms over my chest. "I'll always give you my opinion. Let me know. Whatever you need."

Her face breaks into a grin that's pure sunshine. She bounds to her feet and throws herself into my arms. I catch her against me, and it steals my breath. She clutches at me, laughing, and I lean to rest my chin on her head, allowing myself to smell her shampoo, to hold her for this moment.

She glances up at me. "You're the best. You know that, right?"

"Yeah. The best." I manage to smile, but I'm not sure how. I need to get away from her immediately. "I'm glad you're okay. I'm going to go rescue Colt from Tressa."

"Tricia."

"Right." I point at her, backing away. "Whatever."

"See you on campus in a few days." Classes begin on Thursday, but I promised my father I'd stick around until Wednesday so that I could get a couple more days in with him.

I beat a hasty retreat and duck into Mr. Carmichael's office. There aren't any lights on in here, but the moonlight from the windows is enough for me to find my way to the door.

I pause, though, to look back out on the deck. Shea's got her knees tucked to her chest and stares out at the water. Her sketchbook is on the bench next to her, and it tugs at my chest, dragging a grin to my lips. She always has a pad of paper nearby. When she doesn't, she covers napkins or paper towels with doodles.

How the hell am I going to stand by and watch her hook up with someone new? Shaking my head, I turn from her, slipping out of Mr. Carmichael's office and into the hall before she catches me staring at her. I need to get it together before anyone sees me. The hall is empty, so I run my hands through my hair and gaze up at the ceiling.

After she broke up with Justin, I assumed the hardest part would be watching her heart break over him. But that hadn't been difficult. She hadn't even been the one to tell me they'd broken up. I found out from Colt a couple of weeks after the fact. "Cheated," he'd told me.

They'd been having problems—I'd known that much—but I hadn't asked a lot of questions. I preferred not knowing to knowing too much.

I saw her right before the semester ended, at a bar with her friend Violet. If she was heartbroken, she hadn't let on. That was when I realized that I wasn't really close enough to her that I'd know what her heartbreak would look like. We didn't confide in each other about our relationships. I never wanted to hear about Justin, and she never asked about the girls I saw. Granted, I never have real relationships. I'm not a monk. Girls like me. I'm a good listener, and I pay attention—in and out of the bedroom. But Shea never needed to know any of that. If she heard about it, she never really let on.

It had worked. At least, I thought it had worked.

Now, I'm going to have to watch her find someone new, in front of me. At least Justin had the courtesy to go to a different college.

Needing to move, I set off to find Colt.

Poor guy's still trapped near the dessert table with the middle-aged lady talking about hockey stats. When he sees me, his eyes widen. That's a please-help-me look if I've ever seen it.

Smothering a laugh, I join him, slinging an arm over his shoulder. "Excuse me, ma'am, but Colt's sister is looking for him." I smile, and she gazes up at me, blinking.

"Oh no. I've been talking your ear off, keeping you from your family." She pats his arm. "Go on. I'll be rooting for you and the Tyrants this year."

"Thanks, Mrs. MacFarland. I appreciate that." Colt hugs her, drops a polite kiss on her cheek, then follows me out of the room. "Fuck, man. Left me there long enough. Some wingman you are."

I laugh. "Sorry. I went to check on Shea."

Concern darkens his face. "She okay?"

"Yeah. Too people-y here." I shrug. "It's Shea." We both know she's not one for large groups.

He nods. "Right. Is she looking for me, really?"

"No. She's on the back deck, drawing."

"Okay." We both know she likes to be alone when she sketches. "Come on. Let's go find a drink."

We head out to the patio. It's well past dark, and the family crowd has gone. The music is still playing, and a few couples are sitting around on loungers and chairs, chatting. We hit up the bar. He steps away, handing me a craft beer. We clink the necks together and take deep sips.

"What a fucking night," he says.

That about explains it. I take another drink.

"Shea's okay, though?" he asks.

"She's fine, I think." I consider. "For a girl whose recent ex showed up engaged, she's taking it pretty well." That hadn't occurred to me until right now.

"Yeah. I noticed that. I mean, she didn't come back to the party very quickly, and she waited until he was gone. But she seems more... uncomfortable than broken up."

"Agree." I pause. "You think she's okay?" I've never dated anyone I cared about enough to be too upset about it ending. But worrying that Shea's hurting and we aren't helping upsets me.

"I think so." He sighs. "I think it fell apart a long time before she finally let it go. A friend of mine who goes to school with Justin told me he spent the majority of the spring semester fucking his way through the Tri Delt house."

I growl. "Does Shea know?"

"She guesses, probably. I don't know how much she knows. But it's enough." He shakes his head. "I don't know why she didn't cut him loose years ago."

"She's like you."

He glowers at me.

"Loyal, I mean."

His brow wrinkles as he considers that. "You're probably right."

We lapse into companionable silence. Finally, I inhale. "She asked me the strangest thing." He drinks, cocking his head at me. "She wants me to help her find a date to some charity thing in a couple months."

He wrinkles his nose. "The gala?" He waves his hand. "It's not a big thing. I think I'm in town that weekend. I should be able to go."

"I don't think it's only a date to that, though." I take another sip then laugh but not because it's funny. "I think she's looking for a new boyfriend."

He shakes his head. "No. She's looking for a new hookup."

I gag, choking on my beer.

He pats my back. "You okay?"

I wave him off. "Fine," I gasp.

"She told me earlier that she doesn't want a boyfriend."

"Jesus." If she told Colt that, she's dead-ass serious. I can't even imagine any of my sisters confiding something like that, but Shea and Colt are close.

"Yeah." He shakes his head. "She said something about how she wanted to focus on herself this year at school. Something like that." He narrows his eyes at me. "You'll keep an eye on her, right?"

"She asked me to help her find a date."

He's going to be pissed or concerned. Something. Instead, he smiles. "Perfect."

Not what I expect. "What?"

"I don't know. But that makes me feel better." His grin widens.

"That I'm matchmaking your sister?" He's lost his shit.

"No. That you'll be there to make sure that she doesn't get mixed up with the wrong kind of guy." He picks at the label on his beer bottle. "When she started dating Justin, I was already gone for juniors. If I'd been there, she wouldn't have gotten tangled up with him. Maybe she wouldn't have wasted so much time on him." He smiles, patting me on the back. "But now, I know she'll be okay. You're there. You'll take care of her."

I can only nod. "I'll take care of her." It's true, but God help me. I have no idea how I'll come out on the other end.

Shea

WHEN I ASKED IF Linc could stop over to help me move a desk up to my apartment the next weekend, I thought he would be alone. But when he parks down the street, all four doors of his old sedan open.

I have no idea how these four guys fit into Linc's compact car. I don't even know how Linc drives the thing. With legs as long as his, he should need to sit in the backseat to even use the pedals comfortably. Squeezing another guy over six feet behind him must defy some law of physics.

I recognize two of the guys with him. One is Declan Mitchell, a Chesterboro University playboy and one of Chesterboro's best wingers. But a lot of sports commentators believe that he was good only because of the steadying influence of Cord Spellman, last year's captain and the center on his line. Lots of bloggers and journalists are wondering if he'll be too much of a wild card this year, now that Cord has graduated and gone on to play for the New Jersey Jaguars.

Declan can come off strong, but I've always liked him. He's got a huge personality, but the times he lets it slide, I get the feeling he's got a good heart.

The other guy is Griffin Parker. He's a junior, I think, and the team's enforcer. I hear he does MMA or something at a local gym. I don't know him that well, but Linc must think he's okay because he's rooming with him this year.

The last one isn't familiar, but I assume he's Linc's other roommate. I know he told me his name, but I can't remember it.

The four of them are the kind of hotness that stops girls in their tracks. Literally. Right now, there's a girl unloading stuff from her car, staring at them from across the street. They're all tall, so they definitely stand out, but it's not only that. They're also in incredible shape. Wide shoulders stretch their shirts, tapering to slim hips and the kind of amazing asses and thighs that hockey players are known for.

I would know. I've been around hockey players my whole life.

I admit it's distracting. Objectively, though, Linc's the best looking of all of them. With his shaggy hair and green eyes, he's the hottest guy I know.

I sigh, pushing that aside as I wave. "Hey guys."

Linc tucks his hands in his pockets as he sidles up, the rest of the guys behind him. "Hey, Tiny." He grins, showing off his irresistible dimple. "Where's this desk?"

"It's not that big, you know." I wave to the four of them. "All this muscle? You guys are overkill."

Declan pauses on the street, flexing like he's in a bodybuilding competition. I laugh as Linc shoves him and says, "I told Declan that I was coming here, and suddenly, I had a car full."

"I'm not missing a chance to check in at the Convent." He snorts. "And neither are these stiffs."

I glance behind me. I've rented the last two years at the Covenant Apartments, lovingly nicknamed the Convent because it's an all-girl facility. Technically on campus, it's made up of suites, and it's perfect for me. I had a roommate my freshman year in one of the dorms, but I was out of town so much that we barely had a friendship. Sophomore year, I chose to live alone and have since.

"I'm sure the Convent girls feel blessed by your presence." Griffin shoves Declan, and even at his height, Declan shifts under the force. "But I doubt they're having lesbian orgies right in the hallway, Mitch."

"How do you know?" Declan fires back. "And if they are, you don't want to miss that, do you?"

Griffin rolls his eyes and crosses his arms over his massive chest.

Linc shakes his head and shrugs at me, and I can only laugh. I actually adore the hockey boys. They're not always appropriate, but they're good guys. I've missed them over the summer.

"Shea, this is Ashton Draper. He's new to the team this year and our fourth roommate." Linc jabs a thumb toward the guy I don't know.

I smile at him. "Hi, Ashton." I offer my hand, glancing between the rest of them. "I didn't know they allowed freshmen to live off campus."

"It's Ash," he says, shaking my hand, his smile open and friendly. "And I'm not a freshman. I'm a junior. I played my first two years in Florida. I transferred here this year."

"Ash is a center, a damn good one. He's going to play where Cord did on my line." Declan tucks his hands into his back pockets.

"Those are big shoes to fill, but I'm happy to be here." Ash rubs the back of his neck.

"Welcome to Pennsylvania, then," I offer, but I'm sure I sound skeptical. I mean, we're in the mountains in the northeast part of the state. All of us are in pants already, and it's barely September. There are trees already changing their colors. It's a far cry from the beautiful weather in the South. "I mean, it only rains or snows here *most* of the time."

Ash laughs. "I brought boots."

"Smart. Come on. I'll show you guys the desk. Thanks for coming to help me out." I buzz the door mechanism, and we all go in. There are four boxes stacked against the wall.

"What kind of desk is that?" Linc asks.

"It's a drafting desk. For my architectural drawing." This year's coursework requires a lot more drafting than in years past, so I splurged on a top-of-the-line drafting desk and an accompanying high stool.

"It's not together." Linc puts his hands on his hips, scowling at me.

"No. It's new," I shoot back.

"I didn't bring my tools." I can already see his mind racing. Of course. I should have thought of that. I hold up my hand.

"I have tools." His brow furrows, so I clarify. "I'm going to put it together. By myself. On my own. It's not that big." After my breakup, I decided that it was time I started managing myself. That includes doing things I can do myself on my own.

He shakes his head. "No way. I'll run back to the apartment, grab my stuff. I'll be back."

"Linc, listen. I got it. I'm training to be an architect. I read plans all the time. I can do this." I drop my hand onto his arm. "Just help me get it upstairs."

He scowls at the boxes then at me. But he nods, and together, he and the guys lift all the boxes. "Where's the elevator?"

"No elevator in the Convent." I offer an apologetic shrug. "Stairs this way. I'm only on the second floor."

To their credit, they don't complain, but there's grunting and "oomphs" on the way up the stairs. Still, what would have taken Linc and me three trips only takes them one. I thank them repeatedly.

When all the boxes are in, Linc glares down at them with his legs apart. "Let's get this together for you."

"Oh no." I hold up my hand. "I told you. I can do it."

"I'm sure you can." He pats my shoulder, and the contact sends a wave of warmth through me. "But we're already here. It would be rude not to let me help." He gives me an angelic smile.

I frown at him. The whole rude-not-to-let-him thing is a low blow. My mother abhors anything unpleasant or rude, and he's sending a reminder that she'd disapprove of me scoffing at his help. "You're right," I grit out. "That would be rude."

I swear he looks too smug right now. "Do you have a knife or something to get into these boxes?"

I sigh. I should know better than to argue with him when he's like this. "Fine, but I'm in charge of reading the instructions. You can do the manual labor." I hand him the shears from the box that still has all my supplies in it.

He rips into the box and blows a raspberry. "Instructions? Please. I'm no amateur."

"Don't be such a guy. We're reading the instructions."

"Tiny, I am a guy," he fires back.

I definitely don't need the reminder. I pause, glancing over him. In his jeans and gray T-shirt, he's all male in a way that has always set me a little off-balance. To distract myself, I reach down and snag the packet of screws that also holds the instructions. "You can stay if we follow the instructions."

"Fine," he concedes. "You're the supervisor. We can do the grunt work."

"Perfect. Grunt away."

Griffin steps back. "Dude, I'm tapping out. I suck at this stuff. I put an IKEA bookshelf together once." He shivers. "The exhibition game between Minnesota and Seattle is on." He points at my widescreen television on the wall. "Mind if we watch?"

"I'll join you," Declan says, dropping on the couch. "I don't take directions well."

"You're a hockey player," Linc fires at him. "How's that possible?"

"I make up for it by being really physical at the right times." He winks at me, and I laugh.

"Dick," Linc mumbles, leaning over the boxes, but there's no heat in it. Declan blows him a kiss.

"I'll help," Ash offers. "I help my mom with this kind of stuff all the time."

"Cool." Linc starts pulling out all the packaging. "Let's get this going."

The place is cramped with them in it. The suites in the Convent are really lofts with kitchenettes. I haven't been able to go shopping yet, so I don't have much food. I bought a cookie mix earlier and made those, but that's not enough food for the four guys in my living room. I grab my cell phone. "I'm ordering pizza. There are some sodas in my fridge if you want any."

There's a chorus of half-hearted denials, but I hold up my hand. "Please. Don't pretend you're not hungry." It would be a lie. If these guys are like Linc and my brother, they can eat anytime, anywhere.

That shuts them up. I grin while I call in an order.

By the time I get off the phone, Linc and Ash are in a heated discussion. I snatch up the instructions and step between them. But I'm barefoot, so I don't even reach their shoulders. "What's going on?"

"The packaging said that tools were included." Linc holds up an Allen wrench. "Tell me, is this 'tools'?"

"Um..." I glance between them.

"That's not a 'no,' Reynolds," Ash fires at him.

"It's not a 'yes' either." He throws his hands up in exasperation. "She's basically declared herself Switzerland."

"I'm not Swiss," I offer. "I'm Scottish." I shrug. "And Southern. Whatever my mother's people were, the Southern was stronger."

Linc narrows his eyes at me. "Really? Whose side are you on here?"

"The Scottish side," I say. "And Southern."

"Scottish, huh?" Declan has made himself at home in my kitchenette, scavenging. "Does that mean you know about Scotch?"

"Sorry." I shake my head. "My dad drinks bourbon."

"What's the difference?" Declan asks.

I open my mouth to explain, because my father would be traumatized to hear this nonsense, but Linc puts his hand on my arm and shakes his head. I let it go.

What follows is more of the same, lots of ball busting and goofing off. It takes way longer to put the desk together than it should, but I'm so glad to have them there. Coming back this year, I worried about how many people I really knew and how many were my real friends. Apparently, these guys are still mine.

By the time the pizza gets there, we're about done. When the buzzer sounds, I stumble to my feet and break for the door before anyone else tries to beat me. I didn't pay when I called, and I want it to be my treat. "Be right back."

I skip down the stairs, push through the door to the lobby, and almost run someone over.

"Shea? Is that you?" He steadies me. It's a guy from my biology class last spring. We were the only two juniors in the entry-level class, trying to fill our liberal arts requirements. He helped me out with a few labs when I missed class to see Justin.

"Richie. How are you?" I offer him a hug. "What are you doing here?"

His arms stay around me too long. "My little sister is a sophomore. She's living here this year."

"I've lived here since sophomore year too. It's a great building." I step out of his grasp and rock back on my heels.

"Then I'll see you some this year." He smiles. "Unless you'll be out of town seeing your guy."

The words don't hurt as much as I expect them to. "Nope." I let my lips pop. "No more guy out of town."

"No way." His eyes light up, and he squeezes my hand. "Well, then maybe we can get together for coffee or something."

I can only blink at him. "Are you asking me out?" It's been so long since someone has asked me out, I'm not sure I recognize it.

"Only if you want to go." He nods solemnly.

I try to remember what I know about him. Richie Patterson. I think he's in the drama department. I only remember him as being a nice enough guy to sit next to in biology. But isn't this exactly what I planned for this year? To meet new people, have fun? "You know what, sure. Coffee sounds great." I smile.

He texts me from his phone so I have his number, and we agree to get together soon.

"See you later," he says, pushing through to the stairwell behind me. That's when I see Linc on the stairs, paused on his way down.

As Richie goes around him, he comes down the last few steps to my side. He watches Richie go up to the third floor. "I was worrying. It's dark, and you were gone for a second..."

"I had class with him last semester." I nudge my head toward the third floor where Richie disappeared. "He asked me for coffee." The silence is uncomfortable. "Do you know him?"

"Richie something." Linc's face is unreadable. We'd been having so much fun upstairs, joking around while they put the desk together. But now he's serious, closed off. He glances over his shoulder. "I don't know anything bad about him."

I nod. Right. Because I asked him to help me vet my dates. I'm still kicking myself for that. I should have kept my mouth shut. "Great. That's good."

"I'll grab the pizza for you." He points at the door, where a delivery guy stands outside the glass with three boxes of pizza.

"Thanks."

He nods, greeting the pizza guy and relieving him of the boxes. Then he heads upstairs without another word. I pay for the pizza then follow him.

Linc

"THIS IS THE WORST cookie I've ever eaten." Griff gags, spits out the bite he took, and crumbles the rest of it into one of the napkins Shea had given us. "How is it possible to make a cookie taste this bad?"

I try not to laugh, keeping my eyes on the road as I drive us home. After we killed the pizza, Shea started yawning, so we bailed. But she sent the cookies she'd made home with us.

I let the guys dig in. I've known Shea for almost a decade—she's no baker. "I think she said she used applesauce instead of oil, and I know she doesn't like eggs."

Griff wrinkles his nose. "My God. Poor unsuspecting cookies." He searches around like he's looking for somewhere to hide the napkin and settles on a takeout cup someone left in the back earlier.

"Her mom was a debutante. She's very adamant about stuff like this, and she passed that shit to Shea." I tick them off with my fingers. "Don't show up uninvited. Never show up empty-handed."

Declan cuts in. "We went to her place."

"And"— I lift my last finger as if he hadn't spoken— "always have something to give to guests."

He holds up his half-eaten cookie, studying it like it's a science experiment. "It's not *that* bad." He takes another bite, chewing thoughtfully. "Like biscotti but harder... and not as sweet. And not as good, actually."

I chuckle. Ash doesn't even bother. He puts his back in the box. "Pass."

Declan pops what remains of his in his mouth. "I think it was nice of her. She didn't have to do that."

I shrug. "It's Shea. Of course it's nice." My mind returns to the guy in the stairwell, Richie. I was being honest—I don't know anything about him, really. Drama major, I think. Friends with one of the girls in Violet's sorority. He was at one of their formals last year that I also attended. Seemed nice enough at that party. Scrawny, though. Definitely not an athlete. Tries to give off that cerebral vibe.

He probably doesn't deserve the heap of shade I'm mentally giving him. In his defense, it's not his fault I don't think he's a good fit for Shea. He's probably a nice guy, like I said. But while Shea might be artistic, she isn't a drama kind of girl. They're not going to mesh.

As always, though, I can't tell whether that's the truth or if I'm going to dislike every guy who shows any interest in her.

"So, what's with you two?" Griff puts the lid on the cookies and tucks the box between him and Ash in the back seat. "You guys grew up together? You're friends? You dated?" Griff is a junior, but this is only his second year on the team. He redshirted his freshman year, so I didn't have much of a chance to get to know him. When Declan and I were looking for another roommate in the spring, he vouched for him. If Declan likes him, he's cool with me.

That's probably why he doesn't know much about Shea and me. "She's my best friend's twin sister."

"Oh." Griff nods knowingly. "So definitely never dated."

I snort. He lifts his eyebrows for confirmation, and I shake my head. "Definitely not."

"What is the story, then?" Ash's question is casual, but it sets me immediately on guard. At her place, he watched her too closely, his eyes on her a little too long. "It's obvious you guys are close."

"She's my best friend's twin sister. That's the story." My jaw's so tight it hurts. "At least that's all the story you need."

He obviously doesn't get the message, because he continues. "She have a boyfriend?"

I grit my teeth. "No. She just broke up with a guy she's been dating since high school. This is her first year at school without him."

Declan wiggles his eyebrows. "She could be looking for a rebound, then. Bet I could help her out." He gives me a punch on the arm.

I don't laugh. Nothing is less funny. "Not unless you want my foot up your ass. Shea's a good girl, not a puck bunny or a party girl. Steer clear of her." I pause to look each of them in the eyes as we park.

I hold Ash's eyes a minute longer than everyone else. Of the three of them, he's the one who seems to show her the most interest. Declan and Griff will respect my request. If I call Shea off-limits, that's it. But Ash is new. I don't know him. I stare him down.

Finally, he lifts his hands in a no-harm-no-foul gesture. "Right, you got it. Look, but don't touch."

I give a stiff nod. "Don't even look." I kill the engine, and we all file out.

That definitely goes for me too. Today, it was so much fun to hang out with her. She's so damn genuine, and while she's not extroverted, she's got a sharp wit. I find myself waiting for her observations, wanting to hear her thoughts. I'm never bored with how her mind works.

She had on a pair of shorts that showed off her legs, and they rode up as she moved around the room, putting the desk together. At one point, when she leaned over to screw something in with the Allen wrench, I sighted a strip of skin across her stomach. I needed to get up and visit the bathroom for a minute to get my thoughts together.

She's not my girl to watch, not mine to dig into her thoughts and feelings. As much as I want to hear everything that passes through her head and see every inch of the skin I've only ever dreamed of, she's not for me.

I need to remember that. So as much as Richie and his skinny limbs don't feel like the right choice, I'll keep my mouth shut and keep my eyes—and definitely my hands—to myself.

We head toward the front door of our apartment building. Griff holds up the box of cookies. "What should I do with these?"

"Throw them out?" I suggest. "I'll tell her we ate them and send her our thanks."

"Keep a couple." Declan shrugs. "They're pretty hard. We may be able to use them in practice. As pucks." He offers an awful martial arts move. "Like *Karate Kid*. Soft hands, that kind of thing."

Griff shoves him. "That's *The Mighty Ducks*, tool. And it was eggs."

He winks at him. “No eggs in those, pal,” he says, patting the cookie box.

I laugh as they wrestle it out in the lobby before we head up to our apartment.

Shea

I PARALLEL PARK IN front of a coffee shop ten blocks from campus. I've never been here, but there's a neon outline of a coffee mug blinking in the window. I gaze through the window of my car, feeling hopeful. If coffee's involved, it can't be that bad.

Richie suggested this place for our date. As far as I know, it could be some happening place in Chesterboro that I've never heard of. I've spent a lot of time out of town, and I'm a bit clueless.

I'm about to turn off the car when my Bluetooth picks up my phone ringing. The screen in my dashboard says it's my boss from my summer internship, Jackie. I hit the button to connect.

"Jackie, hi. How are you?" I grin. I haven't spoken with her since I got to school, but I sent her the design for the house renovation I was working on when I got to campus. I've been wondering if she had a moment to look at it.

"Shea. I need to tell you that this design..."

There's a pause, and I hold my breath.

"This is your best work to date."

I grin as pleasure and relief fill me. "Do you think so? I'm so glad you like it as much as I did." I had a good feeling about the draft when I sent it to her last week, but it's always nice to get affirmation.

"I'm going to send you a check for this work." I can picture Jackie pacing around in her office in downtown Southampton. The place is always a mess, a testament to her creative mind moving too fast from project to project. She says she works best in chaos.

I shake my head. "Oh no, you don't have to do that. It was part of my internship."

"You already completed all the terms of your internship and more. You sent this to me on your first day of class," she chides.

"But I love that house. I couldn't help it." It's true—I fell in love with the Shaker house when we went to visit it for an initial consultation. It's exactly what I think Hamptons architecture is: beachy, transitional, yet airy and bright. "It wasn't any trouble. I would love to see that design on the house. That's all. I felt as if it suited it."

"Shea, the first rule of business is that you don't give your services away for free." Her tone is mildly censorious. "The second is that when you find someone who adds value to your company, you do everything you can to keep them." She inhales then says, "I'd like you to continue to work for me while you're at school. We can come up with some sort of ad hoc arrangement or something, where I can pay you by project. But I really value your eye. You have an amazing talent for this kind of work."

"Thank you, Jackie. That means a lot to me."

"It's not empty praise. You know that's not who I am."

I do. Jackie is a creative force, but she's also a shrewd businesswoman. I loved working with her this summer. I learned a great deal from her—not only about renovations and preserving historic architecture but about running a company. "I do know that."

"Then what do you say? Will you stay on?"

"I'm not sure," I hedge. "I'm in school, and it's my senior year. My classes will be difficult. I'm not sure how much time I can devote to you and still do my coursework justice." Even as I say the words, the opportunity tempts me. I'm prepared to dig into a whole lot of commercial design this semester. The chance to work residentially fills me with excitement.

"I'm not soothing your ego." An edge of steel enters her voice. "I can really use your help. With your talent, I know that you're going to have a lot of opportunities, but I really hope you'll consider staying on and even coming back to work with me after you graduate."

The words drop like an explosion onto all my expectations for life.

"I know you're Rory Carmichael's daughter, and I know that he wants you to work for him. I doubt he understands exactly how much of a benefit you'll be to his organization, but I do. I know that you won't make as much with me. But you have a knack for this kind of work. I think you would find a lot of satisfaction in it." She allows me a moment to process. "Please consider it."

"Jackie, I..." I don't know how to finish. Since I showed talent with drawing and drafting as a girl, my father and I have talked about how I'll join Carmichael Enterprises, the conglomerate of real estate ventures that he runs. I've never considered anything else.

"You don't have to answer now. I know you'll need to think about this. Hell, I know you'll have a lot of other options." She chuckles. "But why don't we plan to get together for dinner when you're home over Thanksgiving or for the holidays? No matter what you end up doing, I'll be proud of you. I hope we'll remain in touch."

"I would love that." It's the truth. Jackie became more than a boss to me this summer—she was a mentor. I'm just not sure if what she's offering me fits into the life that I have always pictured for myself.

We say our goodbyes, and I hang up then turn off the car. Richie's standing on the sidewalk, staring at my car, probably wondering what I'm doing. I gather my crossbody purse and climb out, locking it behind me. Waving, I smile. "Hi. Sorry about that. I was finishing up a call."

"No problem." He grins back, burying his hands in the pockets of his skinny jeans. He's wearing a beanie on his head and the kind of canvas military jacket that's slouchy in a hipster kind of way. "Did you find the place okay?"

"I did. It's good to see you." This is my first date since I broke up with Justin. I'm not sure what to expect, but I didn't think I'd feel this awkward.

"You too." He motions toward the door. "Should we go in?"

"Great. Yes. Sure." Probably one of those responses would have been fine. I clamp my mouth shut and step through the door he holds for me.

Inside, the place is dark except for a stage toward the back that sports a solitary stool and a microphone. There are small round tables scattered around the room. A coffee bar is set up in the front, and we head there first.

"What's going on?" I whisper to Richie because it's so quiet in here. I don't want anyone to overhear me and think I'm weird.

He leans closer, and I'm overwhelmed by his cologne, something really perfumy. I try not to wrinkle my nose. "They do spoken-word poetry readings here on Friday nights."

"Spoken-word poetry," I repeat slowly. "I've never been." I'm not sure what it entails, but I'm determined to try new things this year. I guess this is one of them.

His eyes light up. "You're going to love it. Let's get our drinks and find a seat. I'm glad we got here early enough that there are still some tables left."

It sounds like Richie is familiar with the process, so I let him take the lead. With my Americano in hand, I follow him to a table near the restroom as the first poet takes the stage.

I'm not sure what the poor guy says, because it's mostly yelling. When he's finished, a handful of people in the audience stand to clap, so it must have moved them. The next person on stage is a girl who doesn't make any eye contact but reads from a wrinkled piece of paper she took from her pocket. Her shoulders hunch, so I don't feel like she's comfortable, and her uneasiness makes me squirm. After a few moments of some of the saddest words I've ever heard put together in that order, she breaks down into tears and rushes off the stage.

I don't think she was done, but I can't be sure, so I politely applaud. When no one joins me, I stop awkwardly.

Richie pretends not to notice as he sips his black coffee.

"So," I start quietly, "do you come here often?"

"Only when I'm not working." Then he looks back toward the stage, and I get the feeling he thinks we shouldn't be talking as another person steps up.

I fall quiet.

This poet begins a list of words. He pauses for effect between each one, and I struggle to figure out what they all have in common. I still haven't come up with anything when he steps down. I clap anyway.

Through the next two readers, Richie doesn't try to make any more conversation. Finally, I touch his sleeve and motion toward the restroom. He nods, and I gather my purse and push into the ladies' room.

Staring at myself in the mirror, I wonder if I don't remember how to date and whether this is really what people do in their spare time. I glance down at my outfit. I'm wearing new boots with a tall heel, and they're pinching my feet. All I really want is to be back in my apartment in yoga pants, curled up with my sketchpad or a book and the pint of Chunky Monkey I bought earlier.

Years of etiquette training from my mother and boarding school weigh on me. I should go out there and stick it through on this date. I expected that it was only going to be coffee, but this is like performance theater. If it's a show, I need to stay through the whole thing. I didn't notice anyone else leaving. Does that mean I'm stuck here until it's all over?

I pull my phone from my pocket and consider my contact list. I really only have two close friends here at Chesterboro, at least the kind of friends I can send an SOS to in the middle of a tragic date. A pang of sorrow hits me as I realize again exactly how much I've missed out on in my college years.

I'll start working on that tomorrow. Right now, I need an escape hatch.

Violet has a sorority function tonight—something to do with rush, I think—so she can't help me. That leaves me with Linc.

I hesitate.

Linc.

It's not that he isn't my friend, because he is. He'd be irritated if he thought I even considered not calling him. Things with him are more complicated than they used to be, though. I'm not sure how or why, but they are.

Still, he's all I have. I pull up his contact and type out a message.

Linc

"WHAT ARE YOU DOING here, son?"

Damn. I hoped that I'd be able to push through this without anyone noticing. Deep down, though, I know there's no way to avoid everyone. Preseason starts in a couple weeks, so the facility is starting to get busy. But of all the people to witness my personal mess, Coach Chandler is potentially the most dangerous. I stiffen as he skates toward me.

"Evening, Coach. Good to see you." I keep my voice casual as he approaches where I'm sitting on the home bench.

"What are you doing in there?" His brows crinkle over too-astute blue eyes.

I glance down. I'm all laced up and ready to skate. But here I am, on the bench, trapped in my head.

Since I got here, I've been telling myself that today is better. This is the third time I've tried to hit the ice since I got on campus, and it's the first time that I've managed to get all the way out of the locker room and smell the ice without breaking into a cold sweat. I don't know whether it's real progress or if I'm playing games with myself, but it doesn't matter. Coach caught me. Now, there's no way to hide whatever shitshow is happening in my head.

He points behind him. "Ice is that way."

I sigh. "Yeah." But I don't make a move to get up.

Coach takes me in, everything I said and everything I haven't said. I hate the pity that colors his features. "What's going on?"

There's no accusation in the question, but it makes me defensive nonetheless. "Just preparing to get out there, sir. That's all."

His eyes brows lift. "How long have you been preparing?"

I take off my hockey gloves and look at my watch. "About a half an hour," I admit.

"I see," he says, and I get the impression that he does see—too much. His eyes narrow. "How long has this been going on?"

I shrug. "Like I said... about a half an hour." I don't meet his gaze.

"That's not what I mean."

I fold my hands and lean on my knees. "All summer."

"You haven't been on the ice yet?"

I feel his shock like the censure it is. I shake my head, and the movement is jerky and uncoordinated.

"I see," he says again. He steps up to the bench area and sits down beside me. We sit in silence, staring out at the empty ice rink in front of us.

I haven't had a lot of conversations with Coach over the past year. After my injuries last fall, I had to balance remaining part of the team and giving them enough space to find some chemistry with my replacement. At first, my friend Cord Spellman took over for me. That turned out to be a blessing in disguise because after the team that drafted him saw tape of him as a defenseman, they recognized the role he could play in their lines and eventually signed him to a three-year contract. But Cord always played center for our team, so he wasn't a long-term solution. His move to defense left a hole elsewhere. Eventually, one of the sophomores stepped up. I was proud of him because he became an integral part of the team, and I didn't want to get in the way of the group dynamic.

But now, I don't know where to start with Coach Chandler. The words get trapped in my chest.

"Have you talked with anyone about it?"

"My dad, but I'm not sure he counts."

He shrugs. "He does. But what about Spellman? Have you called him recently? I bet he'd be happy to hear from you."

I shake my head. Makes sense that Coach would suggest Cord. We were close last year. All I can offer is, "I'm going to his first exhibition game in New York next week."

"And?"

"And... that means he's got other things on his mind."

"You don't think he'd want to hear about this?" He lifts his eyebrows, all skepticism.

I have nothing to say to that. Coach is right—Cord Spellman is a great friend who went through the ups and downs of my concussions with me last year. Never once did he give me the impression that he was too busy for me, even while he worried about playoffs and contracts and fell for Hannah Marshall.

"If you don't want to talk to Spellman, have you tried Mitchell?" Coach's mouth tilts up. "The guy's a lot of talk, but I get the feeling he's a good friend."

"He is, sir." Declan Mitchell might be a player with the ladies, but he's always been there when I need him.

"But you're not going to talk to him about this, either, are you?"

"No, sir. I'm not." Before he can argue, I say, "I don't want to make a big deal about it. All I need to do is push through. Once

I get out there, I'm sure I'll be fine." I say the words with confidence I don't feel. "I only need to get going."

"There's nothing stopping you, Reynolds."

"Only me, sir." I meet his gaze, and I don't know what he sees there, but after long moments, he finally nods and stands.

"I'm here if you need me." He pauses. "As your coach, I'm obligated to point out that we have a psychologist on staff that specializes in working with athletes, if that's your thing." He steps back onto the ice. "I'll check in with you next week."

"Thank you, Coach." No way am I going to talk to a psychologist, but there's nothing else I can say. Now, Coach is one more person worrying about me, which adds to the heavy weight I'm already imposing on myself.

He nods then skates away as my watch buzzes with an incoming text from Shea: *In two minutes, can you give me a call? Two minutes.*

Worry courses through me. Is everything okay? Why does she need me to wait for two minutes? If something was wrong, she'd have called, wouldn't she? I let that thought soothe me as I wait the two minutes. After exactly 120 seconds, I press the button to call her. When she picks up, she whispers, "Mom? Is that you?"

"No..." I draw out, confused.

"Hold on one second, Mom." Her voice gets muffled, and I think I hear her say, "Oh, okay. Let me call you back in a few minutes."

"Okay?" I say, but she hangs up, cutting me off. I sit, staring at my watch. What the hell?

In a minute or so, it buzzes again, and I pick up her call. "Linc. Hi. Thanks for calling."

"No problem. What's up?" She sounds safe and fine, and that alleviates my concern. Now, I'm only curious. "Why did you pretend I was your mother?"

"I was on a date with that Richie guy."

"Ah." My mouth tastes sour. That's right—he asked her out. I put the pieces together. "Not gala-date-worthy?"

"I'm at that coffee shop on Hanover. Big Perks."

I try to remember what I know about the place. "Don't they do spoken-word poetry readings on Friday nights?" One of the seniors last year fancied himself the next Shakespeare.

"You knew about that? How did you know about that, but I didn't?"

I laugh. "You've been busy." My smile fades. I don't like to think about what kept her busy. "Let me guess. Not too many masterpieces there tonight?"

"God, no." She huffs out a chuckle before backtracking. "I mean... I'm sure they were nice enough people, but..."

I laugh at her attempt to be diplomatic. "Shea, I get it." I've never been to the event, but it never sounded like my scene either.

"But Richie is enjoying himself, so I didn't want to make him leave. I told him something came up with my mom, so I had to go." She sighs. "Oh well. I didn't have high expectations. Where are you? You sound strange."

"I called you on my watch. I'm at the rink."

"Are you skating?"

"I'm about to." I squirm, wondering if I lied to Shea.

"You are?" She perks up. "How about I come by? I haven't been skating in years."

"You want to ice skate? With me?"

"Sure."

Most of the time, when Shea and I hang out, it's with other people, in a group. She tags along to sports events or parties, joins us for lunch, stuff like that. I can't remember the last time we hung out by ourselves.

After the desk assembly, I decided that I can't get that close to her. In the past, I've been able to keep some distance—the appropriate amount to keep with one's best friend's sister. I help if she needs me, we hang out in groups, and I keep an eye on her. But this is another story, and I don't know if I can afford to get closer to her.

I must have paused too long, because Shea tentatively adds, "Unless I'm not allowed. Or you're training, and you'd rather be alone. If so, I totally get it. I can go home. I bought ice cream earlier, and I can just—"

"No, that sounds great. I'd love it if you came and skated with me." I cut off her rambling. When she talks that fast, I know she's nervous, and I hate hearing it. As I say the words, they feel true.

"Great. I've got to stop at home. I think I have my skates still..."

"If not, you can borrow a pair here." They run public skating out of our rink as a community outreach. They have rentals.

"Okay. I'll see you soon." We say goodbye, and she disconnects. I lower my wrist, considering the empty ice in front of me.

This is a bad idea. I haven't been able to skate in almost a year. How the hell am I going to do it with Shea here?

Maybe I should run in, get changed, and meet her out front. I can come up with an excuse, some reason why we can't skate.

If I do that, I need to accept that I'm a coward. I would be lying to her, and I would have to face the fact that I'd rather run away than do this. Until now, I've been able to fool myself into thinking that I am only working up to it, that I'm close. If I bail now, I need to consider the possibility that I can't do this anymore.

My jaw tightens. No way. I've loved skating, loved hockey. There's no way that I'm ready to give up. I don't care what my stupid anxiety or paranoia or whatever is going on with me says.

Besides, she sounded so excited. No way will I disappoint her. I can do this. I just need to get out of my own way. But even as I repeat that again and again, I wonder how true it is.

Shea

"Hey, you." Linc greets me in the lobby wearing his warmup suit and skates. With the added height of the blades, he's even more significantly taller than I am. It almost hurts to look up at him. But his shaggy hair falls on his forehead, and his full grin shows off his dimple, and I'm glad I came.

As I ran up the stairs to my apartment to find my old figure skates, I wondered if I should bail. The way he left after we put the desk together felt off somehow. There's something different between us this year. I'm not sure what it is, but it sets me off-balance in a way I don't understand.

Even now, his smile, the way he rocks back on his heels as he looks at me... it sends heat skittering along my skin. It makes my stomach flutter and makes me nervous at the same time. There are people around us for public skate. Some of the women—from teenagers through middle age—are checking him out. But it's like he's only got eyes for me.

Linc's hot. That's nothing new, and it's definitely nothing I've failed to notice. I don't know that he's ever looked at me like this before, though, like he's seeing *me*, not just "Colt's sister." Except... I can't afford to imagine things that aren't there. Not now. My heart took a beating with Justin. I don't want to be with him any longer, but the breakdown of our relationship bruised me and left me feeling shaken and unsure of myself.

Right now, I'm stronger and more like me than I have been in years. I've worked hard all summer and done lots of soul-searching, and I'm in a good place. At least a better place. What I need is friends, support, and to keep traveling this path. I don't want to risk upsetting the balance with Linc, one of the constants that I can depend on in my life right now.

I glance down at the skates in my hand, glad I have something to distract me. "I found them. They were tucked into a Rubbermaid bucket in the back of my closet, but I still have them."

He wrinkles his nose. "How old are those?"

"High school." I shrug. "But they're still my size, so they'll work."

"Come on." He motions behind him. There are two rinks in this facility, and he directs us to the one that isn't hosting public skate. "Let's get you laced up."

We push through the glass doors. It's quieter here, completely empty, with only the sound of the ventilation system to break the silence. He motions me to one of the metal benches where his bag is open. I plop down and unzip the boots I wore to my date.

"Sorry about your date," he says. "You look pretty."

The compliment sends happiness snaking through me. I can't remember the last time someone who wasn't my family has paid me such a genuine compliment. It's been longer than just since my breakup. At the end, Justin spent more time finding things wrong with me than anything else. What I wore, things I said, things I wanted to do... nothing was good enough for him.

"Thanks." I keep my head down, focused on my skates, suddenly shy. "It's fine. I'd never been to a spoken-word poetry reading before. Now, I can say I have."

He chuckles. "That's very glass-half-full of you."

I can't tell whether he's giving me a hard time or being sincere, so I finish lacing my skates and stand. My ankles tilt, and I wobble.

He grips my arms to steady me. "Whoa. Bit of a bender there, Carmichael," he teases.

I stick my tongue out at him. "Bender" is a jab the guys throw at each other, making fun of skaters whose ankles are weak on their blades.

"Shut up. It's been a long time." I'm not sure why it's been such a long time. My brother plays in the NHL. I could have found my way to the ice a million times over the past years.

I shake that aside. "You might have to hold me up out there. I don't want to fall." I didn't learn to skate until after Colt was already well in love with hockey. By that time, he and Linc were friends, and they would go out on the ice with me. Colt or Linc would stay in front of me and skate backwards, letting me lean forward and hold onto their arms. It was better than using the walkers they gave other new skaters. Both of them have always been so sure on the ice.

As he studies me, his face is tight. He's still cupping my elbows, holding me steady. But his expression is pained... or almost scared. It stills me, upsets the equilibrium in me. *What's going on?* "You okay?"

"Yep. Definitely," he answers too quickly. "I would never let you fall, Shea." It's a vow. Where there was something uncertain a moment ago, there's only determination. I don't know what's going on with him, but whatever fear or anxiety I saw is gone. That glint in his eye says that he's solid. Good. Linc's one of the most confident guys I know. I never want to see him unsure.

"I know you wouldn't," I assure him. I step back, out of his grasp, toward the rink and away from the intensity on his face. "Are you sure you're okay?"

"Absolutely." He nods.

I cast a glance his way as I head toward the rink on my shaking ankles. His face is closed. As I step onto the ice, though, I have to stop worrying about him because I need to focus on not falling on my butt.

There's a lip between the rubber surface around the ice and the rink, and I need to step over it. But that requires me to shift my weight from one foot to the other. I steady myself with a hand on the boards as I cautiously put weight on the blade on the ice. It holds, so I lift my back foot and get both of my blades on the rink. I move—only an inch or two, but it upsets my balance, and I need to lean harder on the boards to make sure I don't wipe out. "Whoa."

"Steady, there." Linc's brows dip, and he hops the lip onto the ice in a graceful bound, landing solidly on his blades next to me. His hands fall to my waist. "You okay?"

"I should be wearing a helmet." I laugh. "Having had braces will be pointless if I lose any of my teeth."

"You were cute in braces," he says, but his eyes are on my feet. The words are offhand, but again, there are the butterflies threaded with panic in my belly. "Come on. Let's see if we can get you going." He pauses, making sure I'm balanced on the wall, and then he shifts, positioning himself next to me. He cups my elbows then gives me a reassuring nod. I pry my white-knuckled grip off the wall and turn toward him. He smiles, all encouragement. "Give a push."

I kick off with my right foot, and we start to move—me forward, him backward. He helps, his feet shifting the slightest bit, but it gets him moving. I never understand exactly how they do that. I can barely skate forward, let alone go backwards with the slightest flick of my ankle.

We move halfway around the rink like this without speaking. I watch my feet and keep a death grip on his forearms.

Being this close to him does nothing to alleviate the wave of awareness that's coursing through me. I'm intensely focused on his hands, on the feel of his fingers on me, even through the coat and the sweater I'm wearing. Even as his nearness unsettles me, I'm comforted by his presence in front of me. He's my safety net, a solid force—physically and emotionally. I'm glad I came.

The farther we go around the rink, the stronger I feel on my skates. I chance a glance at him, smiling, "This is really like riding a bicycle, isn't it?"

He doesn't return my grin. His eyes follow the curve of the rink, and he exhales slowly. "It is, isn't it?"

"Yes." I study him. I squeeze his forearms as we continue. "What's going on with you? You're acting weird."

He sighs, shifting his weight a fraction, but it's enough to send us backward faster. "It's nothing now."

"What was it, then?" I scowl at him. It's always been difficult to get things out of him.

His gaze finds mine briefly before sliding away, refocusing on the rink around us. "This is my first time out on the ice since my concussions last year."

"It is?" I try to imagine my brother staying off the ice for a year. I can't picture it. "Why?"

He lifts one shoulder in a shrug. "I don't know."

I narrow my eyes at him. "Yes, you do."

He meets my gaze briefly and then glances away. "I might have had a few... panic attacks."

"What?" I stop and almost lose my balance, which makes me need to lean in to keep from falling over. Linc props me up, but when I stay silent, waiting for him to expand, he lets go, shifting away a few feet.

"I've had a hard time getting back out there." He shrugs again, even as he circles me, picking up speed, almost like he's testing himself out. He skids to a stop, sending snow everywhere. The grin he gives me is like the sun coming up—a burst of light. "But I guess I'm good now. Like riding a bike," he says, winking at me.

"Why didn't you say something?"

He only shrugs.

I wait for him to say more, but he doesn't. I scowl at him. Linc is always the first one to step up to help, but he's not good at asking for it. Finally, I sigh. I'm not going to get anything else out of him, I guess. "Well, then," I say, waving my arm. "I know you're dying to go faster. You don't want to inch along here with me."

He laughs, and then he's gone. I can only watch. I'm always amazed at how fast he and Colt are. I've skated with them before, though it's been a while, but it's surprising every time. He shoots around the boards, so close to the edges that it's frightening, but he's in complete control. Then he zigzags across the rink and stops fast, his blades digging into the ice. He laughs, the deep sound full of triumph and happiness, and I can't help but laugh with him.

He keeps it up for a few minutes, and I move slowly, watching him. I had no idea he was struggling, and I'm sure Colt didn't either. It's just like Linc to keep something like panic attacks to himself. Knowing him, it's way worse than he even lets on.

Emotion closes my throat. I hung out with him some last year, especially in the beginning of the spring semester, as things got really bad with Justin. Why didn't I notice that he was having a hard time? More importantly, why didn't he tell someone? If not me, he should have reached out to Colt. The two of them are like family.

He skids to a stop in front of me. My arms are out at my sides as I struggle to keep my balance. "I definitely think you're okay now."

"Thanks to you." He pauses, catching his breath, his hands on his hips.

"What did I do?"

"You haven't skated in years."

When he doesn't continue, I wrinkle my nose at him. "So?"

"You might fall. But you don't care. You put on your skates and came out here." He shrugs. "It reminded me that it's okay to fall sometimes." It's casual, or at least he means it to be. But there's a strand of something deeper behind the words.

I glance up, meet his eyes, and hold them. "This hasn't been easy for you, has it? Your concussions, I mean." He wanted to play last year and grumbled about not being able to be out there and help the team. But wanting to play and being physically unable to is different than what he describes. This sounds like he thought he might not ever skate again.

He doesn't respond, only drops his eye contact.

Knowing I made him uncomfortable, I try to find a way to smooth over the seriousness. "Well, you said you weren't going to let me fall," I tease. "I had no reason to worry." I lean forward to give him a playful slap on the arm. I must not have been paying as much attention to my balance as I should have been, because I slip, falling toward the ice, my hands out to brace my fall.

I don't see Linc move. But one moment I'm careening toward the ice, and the next, I'm cradled in his arms, less than a foot from smacking my head.

He surrounds me. Pressed against his chest, I'm insanely aware of the miles of muscle on him, the strength in his shoulders. I press my fingers into the firm planes of his chest. My gaze travels up the front of him to meet his eyes. This close, I realize that the green of them is shot through with gold, like a star centered on his pupils. There's concern on his face, and it softens his usually stoic expression into something breathtaking. Stern and steady Linc is hot, but soft and concerned Linc is a heartbreaker.

My heart pounds, but I don't think it's only from my near fall.

"You hurt?" he asks, and I shake my head.

The words are stuck in my throat or somewhere in my chest where my heart is currently beating too hard for me to breathe. The smell of him—warm, spicy, and masculine—is filling my lungs and my head, taking away rational thought or conversation.

His eyes travel over my face as if he's seeking to verify that I am fine.

I clear my throat. "I'm okay." Why does my voice sound like I just woke up? "Really," I add, because I need to say what I can to get him to let me go, to step away. I can't think with him this close.

He nods and shifts. He rights me with no effort, as if my weight is inconsequential. He keeps his hands on my arms until I can stand on my own, and then he lets go and slides away a foot.

The additional space gives me breathing room, but with him gone, I realize I don't want breathing room. I want him to take my breath away over and over.

I look up quickly, and there's a flash of emotion on his face, but it's gone too fast for me to identify it. In its place is the stoic expression he usually wears. "There you go."

I open my mouth to speak. I don't know what I'll say, though, and before I have a chance to spit out words I might regret, I'm saved by someone calling Linc's name.

He glances up and waves. The corner boards are open, and the Zamboni is there. "We need to get off the ice. Wayne needs to run the machine."

I nod, silently thanking Wayne for saving me from myself as we skate off the ice. I don't know what might have come out of my mouth, but whatever it would have been would have changed things, and I don't want that.

I can't afford to ruin things with Linc.

Linc

OVER THE NEXT WEEK, Shea and I fall into a pattern of hanging out, but I make sure it's always with other people. Having a buffer is a good thing. It lets me step back into the friend zone and keep some distance between us, and it allows me to get my responses to her in check. When she almost fell and I snagged her to keep her from smacking her face, it reminded me of all the reasons why touching Shea is always a bad idea. Holding her in my arms was a special kind of agony. She fits there. I don't want to think that, but I do every time I hug her.

She meets me for lunch sometimes. Again, though, it's not only me. The hockey team sits in the same spot every day, and everyone asks her to join us, so it's more of a group effort. As things get busy in our classes, I'm at the library more than I'd like. I'm a business major, and some of the classes require more research than I'd hoped. She and her friend Violet join me sometimes. So do Ash and Griffin, when he's not at the gym where he works. Violet is a business major, too, so we talk things through. Shea ends up chiming in a lot. She's Rory Carmichael's daughter. She's picked up a lot of savvy over the years.

Declan and I spend the next weekend in New Jersey at Cord Spellman's mom's place. Cord's first game for the New Jersey Jaguars, an exhibition at Madison Square Garden, is Saturday. He kills it, but more than that, he reunites with Hannah Marshall, who sings the national anthem. They'd both gone to Chesterboro with us last year, but Hannah left early to go on tour with the Dazed Zealots, an up-and-coming alternative band. Hannah's debut hit is creeping up the charts right now, and she's scheduled to release her first album soon.

I'm glad they worked things out. Seeing my pal so blissfully happy is great, but it reminds me that I've never felt like that. That's probably my fault. The girl that's always on my mind is the one girl I can't have.

As I walk to class the following Thursday morning in the light rain, my phone buzzes in my pocket. I drag it out to see Shea's message. *You up? I have a big ask.*

I call immediately. When she picks up, I say, "What's up, Tiny?"

"Do you have a game or practice this weekend?" She pauses then hurries on. "Or are you going somewhere or doing anything that might keep you busy during daylight hours Saturday and Sunday?"

I consider. "No, nothing that I know of. Practice doesn't start until Monday."

"How about any of your roommates?"

I chuckle. "Shea, what's going on?"

"I need some people to help me out. The bigger the people, the better."

"We should be free. At least some of us. What's up?"

"The girl at Habitat for Humanity thought she posted the volunteer sign up when the semester started. But it didn't really go up until this morning. So far, there are only four people coming on Saturday to help with the project in Hazelton."

"And you want me to help you. And you want me to bring my friends."

She exhales. "Yes."

I laugh. It's not even nine in the morning, and the weather's miserable. But talking to Shea makes me smile. "Sure. I'll send out a text."

"Oh, thank you. They'll sign for service hours, and I'll call the coach, and he can send a photographer. It'll be great PR for the team." She rushes on. "And I'll make sure there's food. And later, I'll get you guys some beers."

"You don't have to do all that." Habitat for Humanity is a great cause.

"You'll be giving up your weekend. And it's a lot of work..." She sounds like she's regretting asking me.

I hate that. I stop her. "Shea, we would be happy to help."

"Thanks," she offers. "I really appreciate it."

I get the details before we hang up, but I can't help thinking about the guilt in her voice, just for asking. Even if I'd said no or we'd been busy, she shouldn't feel bad for asking for something.

Declan, Ash, and I chug coffee at six thirty on Saturday morning, pile into my sedan, and head toward Hazelton, Pennsylvania, about twenty minutes from Chesterboro. Construction vehicles line the street next to a tired house with a Habitat for Humanity sign. We park down the block, and Shea greets us on the sidewalk. Her long hair is tied back in a high ponytail. She wears a blue Habitat for Humanity T-shirt, sneakers, and a pair of shorts that show off her legs, even giving the slightest hint of the curve of her ass.

She hands us a spray can of sunscreen. "It's going to be hot, you guys. Protect yourselves." I spray myself without argument, but Declan tries to play it down, talking about how the ladies love his tan. Shea gives him a stern glance, staring him down until he shuts up and takes the spray from me. She's small but fierce. Ash doesn't even bother to argue. He only waits patiently until Declan's done, then he dutifully covers himself in SPF. When we're all sun protected to Shea's satisfaction, she grins up at us. "Come on. Let me introduce you."

As she's guiding us forward, a Jeep pulls up, followed by a Lexus. They park behind me, and six more of my teammates step out. They horse around, shoving each other, and Shea grips my hand. "Are those your guys?"

I shrug. "You said you needed help." I sent out a mass text message after she called, telling the whole team about Shea's dilemma, requesting help. Declan chimed in that it would be a good team bonding experience, and since Declan's almost certainly going to step into the captain role this year, a lot of the younger guys must have decided to come. I'm glad. The sooner the team creates a rapport, the better our chances of collective success.

Shea beams up at me. "Thank you. This means a lot to me." She hurries to great the newcomers, wielding her sunscreen can. When one of the rookies complains, Declan folds his arms over his chest and says that SPF is important, as if he weren't whining about it a few minutes ago. Sure enough, though, the rookie applies it without any more complaints.

She herds us all down the street to where an official-looking woman in a Habitat for Humanity hat and polo shirt is holding a walkie-talkie and a clipboard. Shea motions toward our group and says, "Kyla, this is the Chesterboro University's ice hockey team. I told them we needed help, and they wanted to step up for us."

Kyla looks us over, and her jaw drops as her eyes go wide. I glance around at the ten of us. Alone, each of us is big and probably intimidating. In a group, we're overwhelming. To her credit, though, she quickly shakes her head. "Hi, guys," she offers with a tentative smile. "Thanks for coming out. We'll definitely be able to use your help."

She separates us into groups, sending a few of us to different places in the house. What looks like chaos outside is quickly sorted, and in a matter of minutes, we set off to do what's necessary.

Shea's right—by mid-morning, the sun is bright outside, and the inside of the house is a sauna. Everyone's drenched in sweat, but the tone of the project remains upbeat. Something about working on a task sure to improve someone's life makes everything easier to tolerate.

After spending the middle of the day outside on the roof, repairing rotten plywood and helping to install shingles, I get sent inside to help install a new wall between the kitchen and the living room. Shea's there with the architectural engineer, reading the plans and directing people to make sure that the measurements are correct. I jump right in, following her instructions and lending my muscle where it's needed.

I've witnessed Shea in a lot of different situations. When we were younger, she was Colt's pesky sister, always tagging along and getting on her brother's nerves. She's been the loudest cheerleader at his games, decked out in team gear, her face painted. I've watched her as Justin's girlfriend... But I've never watched her this way.

Here, seasoned contractors are asking her opinion, turning to her for her input. Huge construction workers lean down to hear her better over the saws and nail guns and endless conversation.

I've always loved the sounds and smells of a work site, and it's obvious she loves them too. Her eyes are bright, her shoulders are back—every part of her is engaged. I keep positioning myself nearer to her, so I can listen to her comments and hear her take on how things are going. Or maybe I just always want to be where she is.

I volunteer to help the others, who are nailing in the boards for another wall between the kitchen and the dining room. They made the kitchen larger to accommodate modern appliances.

I'm holding a board level when the guy above me on a ladder bumps his nail gun, and it falls right toward Shea, who's measuring the jam to make sure it meets her specifications.

I don't think but dive toward her, snatching her against me. I curl my body around her and shift so that the nail gun bounces off my left shoulder.

Pain laces along my back and down my spine, and I grunt, but I hold her tightly and keep moving away from it as it clatters to the ground beside me and shimmies to a stop.

The place erupts into concerned shouts, but I can only think about Shea. "You okay?" I grit out, purposely ignoring the pain vibrating through my shoulder. All I can think about is the terror coursing through me. Did the nail gun hit her on the way by? Did I not get to her in time?

"Oh my God," she gasps. "Your shoulder. The nail gun. You're hurt..."

"Are you hurt, though?" I ask again, scanning her face for any sign that she's injured. I can't find anything. Her skin's still perfect, her eyes are clear, and her mouth...

"I'm fine," she whispers. "You got me."

Relief explodes in my chest, and I can breathe again. I force myself to loosen my grasp. Her hand stays on my arm. "Are you okay?" she asks.

I rotate my shoulder, moving my arm to take stock of the damage. I've played hockey long enough to have a good guess of when I'm really hurt and when I'll just be black and blue tomorrow. "I'm okay."

She ignores me. "Kenny, I'm going to take Linc to the first aid tent. I'll be right back."

"I'm fine, Shea." Now that the immediate threat has passed, I wonder how much I've given away, throwing myself on top of her like a fucking knight in shining armor. Already, I sift through the ways that I can downplay what I did. "It didn't hit me hard. I'm a giant. I didn't want it to hurt you."

"I was there, Linc." She stops in the foyer, scowling up at me. "I know what happened. Are you going to pretend like I didn't see what I saw?" She narrows her eyes then grabs my arm and drags me outside again. I follow her to the first aid tent, and she stops me in front of an EMT. "Hi, my friend got hit in the shoulder with a nail gun?"

The guy is immediately ready. "You got a nail in the shoulder?"

"No," I specify. "A nail gun fell and hit me on the shoulder."

He visibly relaxes. "Okay. Let me look at you."

What follows is a quick and efficient physical exam. Shea steps out of the tent to give me some space, but I can see her pacing nearby, her sneakers moving back and forth. Finally, Mr. EMT hands me my T-shirt and says, "I suspect you'll only have a nasty bruise. If anything worsens, I'd go and get it X-rayed, though."

"I'll stop by the trainer at the rink on Monday." I shrug into my shirt.

"Good plan." He hands me an ice pack. "Hot and cold, off and on. I'm sure you know how this goes."

He means icing and heat to treat a bruised muscle. I nod. "Got it."

"Is everything okay?" Shea looks me over with the same calculated gaze she gave the design plans inside, as if she needs to make sure that all the pieces are in the right spot.

"Like I said. Bruised. I need to have one of the trainers check me out on Monday." I head toward the house, determined to get back to work and to get her to stop looking at me like that—too intensely.

"Then you shouldn't come back tomorrow. What if it's hurt worse than you think?" She worries her bottom lip, catching it between her teeth.

I stop her. "Shea, I'm fine. It wasn't a big deal at all. Anyone else would have done the same thing." I need to believe that she would have been safe if I wasn't there and that I'm not unhealthily consumed with where she is all the time.

She glares at me. "You got hurt saving me."

I scowl back. "You're making too big of a deal out of it. I'm just glad I got there in time."

Anger flashes across her face. She puts her hands on her hips. "It is a big deal. Why are you playing it down?"

Because I have to. But I keep my fucking mouth shut. Better silence than saying something stupid.

"How did you get there so fast? I don't think anyone else knew it was happening, and you had already jumped in and saved the day." She stares up at me, waiting, needing an explanation.

I scan her beautiful face, taking in all the worry, all the confusion. The trace of guilt. She wants to know what happened —to understand why I'm hurt and she isn't. I should lie, but I can't. Not when she's looking at me like that. Instead, I utter words that prove how truly damned I am: "Tiny, I can't help looking at you."

Shea

I CAN'T HELP LOOKING at you.

Saturday night, I go to a party with Violet. It's at one of the fraternities that I don't know well, but Violet's sorority sisters are there. When we get there, I look over the crowd and assure myself that no hockey guys are there before I relax. Though it's not *all* the hockey guys I'm avoiding. Only the one.

I can't help looking at you.

Violet does shots with her sisters, so I sip on a beer then switch to water. I'm going to be back at the Habitat house tomorrow, so a hangover shouldn't be in my future. Besides, Vi broke up with her boyfriend, Nate, right before school started. He went off to training camp in Toronto and gave her some now-isn't-a-good-time-for-either-of-us-to-be-attached bullshit. She's taking it hard.

I make small talk with some of the brothers. A few of them even hit on me. This is what I'm supposed to be doing—going to parties, meeting people, and being a typical college girl. Except all the pickup lines and compliments feel fake. All I keep seeing is Linc's sincere expression as he tells me that he can't help looking at me.

I can't get it out of my head.

He practically gritted the words out at me, though, and then headed right back into the house as if nothing had happened. I watched him go, and those words—possibly the most romantic words anyone has ever said to me—streaked warmth and awareness through my whole body.

When I got back inside, he was already busy hanging sheetrock. I tried countless times to make eye contact with him, but for a guy who claimed that he couldn't help watching me, he did an admirable job of ignoring my efforts.

I've rolled the whole episode around in my head on repeat. By the time I get Violet into her room and find my way to mine, I've convinced myself that he didn't mean it the way it sounded. He meant to say that he couldn't help looking *out* for me. He said the words so factually, as if the certainty of them would never be in question, and I'm absolutely sure, with every fiber of my being, that he will look out for me. That was what he must have meant.

Except, as he stared at me, all I wanted was for him to mean them—*really* mean them.

I roll around in bed all night, struggling to get comfortable before I fall asleep at dawn.

My mother's ringtone wakes me shortly after that. "Good morning, sweetheart. I thought I'd catch you on your way to the Habitat site."

I check the alarm clock. Damn it, it's already after six. I'm running late. "I'm not in the car yet. I'll be leaving in a few minutes." I bound out of bed, tucking my phone between my shoulder and my ear, and hurry around the room, searching for clothes. "Good morning, Mama."

"I'm going to be setting seating for the gala today with Melanie. I wanted to find out who you planned to bring with you."

I wiggle into a pair of shorts and pause. "I didn't think the RSVPs were due for a couple of more weeks."

"They aren't, baby. We just wanted to get a jump on things."

Her voice is too casual, and I narrow my eyes. "This is your way of asking me if I have a date yet, isn't it?"

"Not exactly..."

That's code for "absolutely." "I haven't decided if I'm going to bring anyone yet, Mama." I sigh. "And I know that it wouldn't be a huge deal to adjust the seating chart if I decide to come alone."

"I only hoped that you'd have someone there with you. That's all."

"I don't need anyone to be there. Colt said he could come, and I can do this on my own if I want to." In the few weeks I've been back to school, I've realized how true that is. I'm a lot stronger than I think I am. "I'm still looking, though," I say before she jumps in to argue. "If I find someone I'd like to invite, I'll invite him. But I refuse to bring just anyone."

"You know," she offers, and I close my eyes, bracing for whatever comes next, "your father was telling me that there's a very smart, up-and-coming analyst in their hedge fund. He's only a few years older than you, and I saw him, Shea. He's quite handsome—"

"Mother"—my voice is sharper than it needs to be—"I do not need you to set me up on any dates."

"Well, if you say so, dear. But keep him in mind. Your father says he's really going somewhere."

If Dad said so, I'm sure he's right. I bite my tongue on any response, though. "I'm running late. I'll call you later. Tell Melanie I said hello."

We say goodbye and hang up. I know my parents and my brother are only looking out for me. I only wish sometimes that all three of them didn't feel the need to smother me. I'll decide when and if I'm ready to date someone. I'm still exhausted from the emotional toll my last boyfriend took.

Shaking my head, I throw my phone in my bag. I need to hurry, or I'm really going to be late getting to the project.

When I arrive at the Habitat job site, the hockey guys are already there. I greet Linc like I didn't spend the night before wondering what he meant. He's in the middle of hanging cabinets in the kitchen, so all I get in response is a nod. Perfectly normal.

I definitely overreacted.

Feeling awkward and off-balance, I set to work painting, planning to drown myself in work. The contractors replaced the HVAC system yesterday, but the windows are open to air out the fumes. It's hot inside, and before long, we're all sweating. Even with my hair in a ponytail and my sleeves rolled, I'm disgusting. After the first coat on the dining room, I take a break. The volunteers have set up a tent with jugs of Gatorade and water, and I head that way. But as soon as I hit the porch I grind to a stop.

Linc must have had the same idea, because he's already there, filling up a paper cup with water. Except he's a guy, so he enjoys the luxury of taking his shirt off to cool down. He's using it to mop his brow.

At the picnic, when he saved me from my see-through dress, I noticed how cut he is. Colt said that he has been spending a lot of time working out and running because he's determined to make a great comeback this year. All that hard work is on display. He doesn't see me right away, so I have a second to admire him. Miles of tanned muscle cover him, and I'm not the only one who notices. Two other female volunteers watch him, too, probably trying their best not to drool.

There's more than a six-pack on his stomach, made more pronounced because his shorts are riding low on his hips. The angles and planes of him are arranged in exactly the right way, and a wave of heat that has nothing to do with the warm weather washes over me, filling my stomach.

He's so hot that it's almost hard to look at him.

One of the volunteers that had been staring at him must have gotten up the guts to go and engage. She's pretty, tall, blond, and curvy. I don't know what she says, but he smiles down at her, all damp and sweaty hair and adorable dimples, and it gets me moving off the porch and toward him even before I catch myself.

"Hey," I interrupt them. "How's it..." My question trails off as he turns, and I see firsthand the damage the nail gun did to his shoulder yesterday. The black-and-blue mark stretches from his neck to the bottom of his shoulder blade. He must have hunched over me and absorbed the entire impact of the machine. "My God."

I step around him and, without thinking I trail my fingers along the bruise, concern and guilt firing through me. He stiffens, jerking away and growling, "What are you doing?"

I retrieve my hand as if I've been burnt. Embarrassment eats at my stomach, and I can feel the heat rising in my face. "Your back is... I mean, you're really hurt."

"It's fine," he cuts me off. "Please don't touch me." The words are harsh, almost angry. I'm not sure I've ever heard him use that tone before.

The girl who had been flirting with him a moment ago shifts her weight, uncomfortable. "I should go," she mumbles, slipping back toward her friend.

I watch her, horrified. Her presence makes this all more awkward. If she hadn't witnessed me touching him like I'm his mother or something, or she hadn't seen his repulsion at my touch, I might have been able to laugh this off. But I can't now. Instead, I nod, swallowing hard. "You're right. I'm sorry."

I spin on my heel, heading back inside. Except there are a lot of people in there. The kitchen's full of people working on cabinets, and there are painters everywhere. I keep going, stepping out onto the back porch. No one is here, so I pause, desperate to gather my thoughts.

I rub my forehead. Why did I do that? I didn't think, that's all. He's hurt because of me, and I hate that, and all I could do was think about what I can do to make it better, but that's silly, because there's nothing I can do for a bruise like that.

So why did I need to touch it, to touch him? I smooth my hands over my hair, staring up at the bright blue sky.

Linc's voice behind me interrupts my thoughts. "Shea, I..."

I close my eyes. "We're good." I force a smile to my lips and face him. He's shrugging into his T-shirt, but it's damp, so it sticks to him, and I hate that I'm noticing how good that looks. "I get it. We don't need to talk about this."

His eyes narrow. "About how I snapped at you? Because I shouldn't have done that, and I'm sorry." He grips his bicep, and it stretches his shirt across his shoulders. Holy heavens, his body...

"I shouldn't have touched you," I fire back. "But I hate that that mark is there because of me. I didn't think." I laugh, trying to lighten the mood, to return things to normal—the normal before I ran my fingers across his beautiful back and he flinched. "I'm like your sister. Obviously, you don't want me touching you."

He buries his hands in his hair. The movement stretches his arms over his head, revealing the ridges of his stomach and showing off the width of his shoulders. "That's not it." He blows out an exasperated breath.

I look him over, unsettled by how I'm feeling, standing so close to him. My heart races, my hands are sweaty, and my stomach feels all fluttery. I got over these feelings for Linc years ago. "Please, Linc. Just go back inside."

He steps toward me. "I can't." This close, he's overwhelming. I'm in sneakers, so he towers over me at his full height, and I'm forced to look up at him. I tremble, surrounded by him. It's hot, but all I can smell is him—spicy, salty, and warm male skin. Desperately, I want to touch him—his arms, his hands—something that will ground me and remind me that I'm steady. But after what just happened, all I can do is stand there, staring up at him, wanting him.

When did this happen? We've known each other forever. His attractiveness has been a fact, like his friendship with my brother. Why is my body reacting like this to him now?

"Why are you making this a huge deal?" I whisper. "You didn't like that I touched you, and I apologized. Can't we just get back to normal?" Because that's what I need. I decided long ago that having him in my life—as my friend, as my brother's friend—is better than having nothing of him at all.

His gaze is hot and intense. His fingers skim my arms in the briefest and softest contact, but it's enough to send shivers of awareness along every inch of me. I inhale sharply, but I stay still, unwilling to move or do anything to cut this short. My lips are dry, so I lick them, and his eyes fall to my mouth.

"You have it wrong," he whispers, his breath soft on my face. "I don't hate your touch. Not at all."

The words steal my breath and send a quiver through me. His gaze rakes my face, and the heat there is enough to burn me. I bite my lip to keep it from shaking, and his eyes find my mouth again. He raises a hand as if he's going to cup my face. Oh, God, I want him to. I've never wanted anyone to touch me more than I want him to right now, and the knowledge sends an earthquake through everything I know to be true about Linc Reynolds.

I want him. To me, he's not only attractive in an all-hockey-players-are-hot way. This isn't how I felt about him as a middle-school girl. This is the person who's always been there for me—through loneliness when Colt left for juniors, through feeling like I didn't fit in at boarding school, and then through my relationship with Justin. He makes me feel strong, and he's there when I need him. I trust him implicitly. Right now, all I want is to feel his hands on me.

"What exactly are you saying?" Not hating my touch is not the same as wanting more of it.

He inhales and then lets the breath out slowly. "I'm saying that you shouldn't touch me." He retreats a step, putting space between us. As I watch, his face firms, and all the intense, raw emotions that lit me on fire earlier are gone, tucked behind the steadiness he's known for. When he speaks, his voice is strong and sure. "And I shouldn't touch you. You and Colt are like family to me."

The message is clear—he's my brother's best friend. That isn't a line he wants to cross.

"Of course," I answer because there's nothing else to say.

Linc

I DON'T TALK TO Shea the week after the Habitat for Humanity project.

Training started that Monday. I've managed to get back on the ice without any more panic attacks, but I'm behind the eight-ball. Though I've done every off-ice workout I can think of—running, hiking, lifting, yoga—nothing works exactly the same muscles as skating does. I spend the first week of practice pushing myself as hard as I can then dealing with aches and pains as my body catches up with me.

For her part, she doesn't come to lunch with us. When I do see her in the cafeteria, she sits with Violet or another girl I don't recognize but who I think is also in the architectural design program. She's got red hair, and her name starts with a *P*, I think.

She waves to me from across the cafeteria, though. She's done nothing to lead me to believe that there's anything wrong. But there is, and it's my fault. I haven't been able to keep the distance I usually do. I got dangerously close to crossing a line with her that should never be crossed.

I wanted to kiss her. If I'd leaned down...

Since we got back to school, I've seen her too much. It's upsetting our equilibrium. I got too close. I need to keep more space, or I'm going to end up doing something really stupid and upset the balance of everything in my life. After a year with the concussions, I'm just getting my life back on track.

On Thursday, I get a voicemail from my father. "Linc, call me back. We're going to be making some adjustments to your mother's treatment, and I thought you should know."

I'm heading to practice, so I dial his cell. He doesn't pick up, and I assume he's at work, so I call home. My oldest sister, Avery, picks up the house phone. "Hey, Ave. How's it going?"

"Linc." I can hear my sister's smile. It's only been a few weeks since I saw her, but I miss her already. "I'm so glad you called."

"Dad left me a message, but I assume he's at work and can't answer."

"Yeah, he and Mom got back from the doctor's a little bit ago, and he needed to go finish things up. He's still pretty busy." Things slow down in the winter months, so I imagine our father is pushing to finish as much as he can before the weather turns. "Hold on, Linc. Let me go outside."

I wait as I hear the back porch door swing open and the door close. "There," she says. "Now, I can talk."

That doesn't sound good. "What's up?"

"What did Dad say in his message?"

Starting with a question. Never a good sign. "He only said that they're going to be making some changes to Mom's treatments."

"Yeah. She's going to start chemotherapy."

"What?" My mother has multiple sclerosis, not cancer.

"Her flare-ups have gotten more and more frequent. You know that. The effects are really taking a toll on her. We know that her MS is going to get progressively worse. They think that if they put her on a maintenance dose of mitoxantrone, it might help her relapses."

"That sounds extreme, doesn't it?" I rack my brain, going over what I know about her treatment options and phases. I haven't been home in three years, at least not extensively. This summer was the longest, and I spent most of it working with my father. Mom was sick a lot, though.

"Things weren't only bad this summer, Linc. Last year was really hard," Avery offers. "I don't think they tell you enough. I've mentioned that you deserve to know, but they want you to focus on college and hockey." She laughs softly. "You know how things are in our family. Make jokes, pretend everything is fine."

"I can still play hockey and take care of my family."

"What are you going to do?" I can almost hear her scowl. "Come home? That's exactly what they don't want you to do."

I know that my parents are my biggest supporters. Even when I got hurt last year and lost my allowance for room and board, they insisted I continue at Chesterboro. My father's exact words were "When you get back out there, you can prove to those assholes how much you're worth."

"How are they paying for this?" They haven't said much to me, but the few things I've gathered is that their insurance isn't that great. My mom works part-time—barely—and my father is self-employed. Not the greatest benefits.

The silence from Avery is deafening. It tells me everything.

"Fuck."

"You can't tell them that I told you all of this," she hurries on. "I know they would have told you themselves if they wanted you to know. You know how proud they are."

"Don't I deserve to know?" Anger flashes through me. Why is my sister the one breaking this to me?

"You do, Linc. But they know you. We all do." Her voice quiets. "You'll want to come home. You'll want to help out. They want you to be there more than they want you to be here."

Her words ring true, even though they piss me off. I'm an adult, for Christ's sake. I should be able to make these decisions on my own. "What can I do?" I ask. Avery is almost eighteen, and since I've gone away to school, she's stepped in where I left off—helping out and shielding our younger sisters the best she can.

"Kick ass at school, big brother. And if you can, kill it at hockey." She doesn't continue, but I read between the lines. I've read the articles about me. There's speculation and rumor that I'm not the same now. Before my concussions, I was one of the best-ranked college defensemen in the league. I'd been drafted by Boston right out of high school, but they hadn't signed me, preferring to let me mature in college and preserve their cap space for a few more years.

After the brain injuries, I'm sure they're waiting to see if I can put a comeback together.

I've felt the pressure all summer, since my neurologist told me that I was good to get back on the ice. But never has the weight to excel felt so heavy. My parents need help. If I can sign an NHL contract, I can do that.

I've never been one to let people down when they need me, and I'm not planning to start now.

"I got this, Ave," I tell her, and I mean it. I don't have the time for pansy-ass panic attacks. Not now. I need to get my shit together. "When's Mom's first treatment?"

"In a couple of weeks."

"I'll try to get home soon." It's still only September. We don't have games until the end of October. I'll check with Coach to make sure I don't miss anything then make the drive home.

"She'd love that, Linc."

"Hold that shit together, Ave," I say, feeling the distance between my family and me more intensely than I ever have.

"Always, you goon."

I chuckle as I hang up then pocket my phone. I'd continued talking as I walked to the rink, and I'm standing outside. I glance up at the building, one hand holding my bag on my shoulder, the other on my hip.

This is my ticket. Hockey. I'm a mediocre student, at best, so I won't be setting the world on fire with my academic-related job prospects. In the back of my head, I always assumed I'd go work for my father after college if things didn't work out with hockey. But we need more money than that right now, and I am in a position to get it.

As I head toward the door, I know one thing for sure. There's no way I'm going to squander my shot.

Shea

AND... HE'S CRYING.

"It's just..." Walter, my date for this evening, sniffs and uses the cloth napkin in his lap to wipe at his nose. "I don't understand what happened. We were going to get married."

I pat his hand across the table, but it's an awkward gesture between two people who barely know each other. "I'm sorry, Walter." I retrieve my hand. I'm not lying. I *am* sorry for his breakup... and for agreeing to this date.

"Thanks, Shea. I appreciate that. And I'm so sorry for breaking down." He inhales a shaky breath and appears to regain some of his composure. I offer an encouraging smile. I hope he's getting it together and we can finish this date gracefully. Maybe I'll even be able to get dessert. The restaurant he suggested, Trello, has amazing cannoli, and I'm dying for one. But as I watch, his eyes fill again, and his shoulders shake. He crumbles in front of me.

I stifle a sigh then slide out of my side of the booth and into his. Stiffly, I wrap my arm around him, and he curls into my side as he weeps. *Poor guy.* "I understand. I mean, it's only been nine months, right?"

"Ten," he gasps.

I rub his shoulder. "Of course, ten. But I'm sure it feels like only yesterday." Robert, our waiter, peers around the end of the seat. I wave frantically at him, gesturing for the check and circling my hand to signal that he should hurry. He nods and bustles off.

No cannoli for me.

"I miss her, Shea. I do."

"I know you do." As I learned through the course of dinner, he and his ex-girlfriend, Lynn, dated for three blissful months until she called it quits before Thanksgiving last year, claiming to need space. "These things can be difficult."

Robert returns with the check in record time then escapes. I use his appearance to return to my side of the table. Still rubbing his eyes, Walter flips open his billfold and stiffens. "Oh my. I didn't bring enough cash for..."

This is already a disaster. I'm not about to haggle over the check with him. I cover the check folder with my hand. "That's fine. I'll get this. Why don't I take care of this while you run to the restroom and gather yourself?"

"Are you certain?" he asks, but he's already shifting to stand.

"Absolutely." I slide the bill closer to me.

His cheeks still wet, he blubbers his thanks then retreats to the back of the restaurant.

I blow out a breath. Reaching into my bag, I retrieve my wallet and drop my American Express card into the folder, closing it with a snap. Leaning back, I press my hand against my forehead and reach for my wine glass, downing the rest of it with a determined tilt. Robert, who has been perennially nearby during the entirety of this fiasco, appears next to me. "Would you like another glass of wine, Ms. Carmichael?"

Yes, desperately. I shake my head and push the check toward him. "No, thank you, Robert. We'll be out of your way in a few minutes." Trello prefers reservations, but there are always people waiting, hoping that someone doesn't show or that there's extra time between diners. I feel bad that I rushed Walter through dinner, but I'm glad Robert can squeeze in another tip this evening.

He smiles, and if I'm not mistaken, there's pity on his face as he hurries off to the register.

When he's gone, I sigh again. Walter asked me to go out on Monday. I don't know much about him, but I agreed. He's in my major and seemed nice enough, and I wanted to forget about Linc and whatever disastrous conversation we'd had over the weekend.

I've been avoiding him. Since he hasn't called or texted, it seems he's returning the favor.

I know I told him that I'd check in with him about the guys I might date. But the gala's only two weeks away, and the chances that I'll be able to find a date are pretty slim. Moot point now.

Besides, I've realized I'm okay going alone. My family will be there, and they're who matter. I don't care anymore about what Justin or anyone else thinks. Colt was right—I'm not the kind of girl who has casual relationships, and I'm certainly not the kind of girl who can sleep with someone I don't care about. Pretending otherwise will get people hurt, and if I really want to depend on myself, I need to learn to stand alone sometimes.

That isn't my problem, though. My real issue is that I can't stop thinking about my brother's stupid best friend. After the Habitat project, I keep replaying Linc and his whole best-friend's-sister moral-high-road speech. Except the way he looked at me... I've never seen anyone look at someone like that before.

At least, no one has ever looked at me like that before. Not even Justin.

Wishing now for that second glass of wine, I check to be sure I have all my belongings so I can hurry Walter out of here when he gets back. Robert sweeps back with the check, to which I add a tip and sign before tucking my AmEx back into my vintage clutch. Then I wait. It feels like I sit there alone for hours as Walter finally shuffles out of the restroom. He looks calm. We can still end this on a respectable note.

As he moves to slide back into the seat, I stand. "The check's all taken care of. Are you ready to go?"

"Oh, um, sure." He nods, waving ahead of him. "After you."

Squaring my shoulders, I weave through the restaurant. On the sidewalk outside, I step away from the waiting line, holding my clutch between Walter and me like a shield. "Thank you for coming out with me tonight, Walter." I smile, extending my hand.

He ignores my hand and folds me into a warm hug. I pat his back. "Thank you, Shea." He pulls back, holding me by the shoulders at arm's length. "I know you recently went through a breakup too. I knew you'd understand what I was going through."

"Right." I extract myself from his grasp and wave. "Thanks again, Walter." I tuck my bag under my arm and hurry around the building and toward the parking lot, allowing the fake smile to slide off my face. When I'm out of his sight, I pull open the clasp of my purse and dig around for my keys and phone. I unlock my car and slide in, turn on the heat, and let my head fall back against the headrest.

This was a mistake. Dating someone else isn't going to distract me from the guy who's really on my mind, even if that guy has made it clear that there's nothing going to happen between us.

The dashboard says that it's only nine o'clock. I'm not going home. I'm in college, for Christ's sake. It's Friday night, and I'm supposed to be partying, having fun. I pull up the contacts on my phone and dial Violet.

"Hey, honey. How was your date?" There's music on in the background.

"Tragic. Shakespearean. Are you going out tonight?"

"Absolutely. Fat Eddie's has a great DJ." Fat Eddie's is a bar right off-campus.

"Can you swing by my place so I can walk with you?" No need for cars to go to Fat Eddie's, and I feel like having a drink or ten. That'll help me forget that I'm catching feelings for Linc Reynolds.

"This is going to be fun," Violet says with a squeal. "See you in a half-hour. I'll text when we're outside."

I disconnect and head home.

Linc

WE WALK THROUGH THE door to Fat Eddie's at midnight. Declan suggested that we go out for some team bonding. Since he got elected captain this week, he's taken his job very seriously. As his roommates and members of the top line, Griff, Ash, and I agree to go, as does the other winger on Declan's line, Hunter. Our presence will lure anyone who's twenty-one or in possession of a decent fake ID here.

The place is packed. Its location close to campus makes Eddie's a popular college destination, but tonight is even busier, thanks to the DJ. I don't know her, but Declan said she's great. They call her Birdie.

She's doing her job—the crowd is heavy on the dance floor. Declan leads us toward the back, where the hockey team usually congregates. It's away from the dancing and the loudest of the music but still a prime location near the bar.

As we're shifting through the crowd, I catch sight of Shea.

She's in the middle of the dance floor. She's next to Violet and a few other Delta Alpha girls, including the redhead I see her with at lunch. But it's Shea who draws my eyes, as always.

What's she doing here? She's supposed to be out on a date with some guy from her major.

Not that she's the one who told me. Violet mentioned it when I saw her at the library yesterday. Whatever happened on the date, though, it must have ended early, because she's here now, dancing. I try not to be thrilled by that. She's supposed to be dating, isn't she? She's supposed to live her life, and I'm not supposed to be in it... at least not like that.

I grit my teeth, unable to look away from her.

She's got her hair down around her shoulders. It's hot in here, so she's wearing something strappy—a tank top or something—and the color is high on her cheeks. She laughs at something Violet says, tilting her head back, and the view of her neck is enough to send awareness through me and tighten up my dick.

Damn it, why is it always like this with her? She's the most unavailable girl, and I can't stop thinking about her.

A low whistle drags me out of my stupid self-pity. Next to me, Ash is staring at Shea and the Delta Alpha girls. "Our Shea looks pretty tonight, doesn't she?"

"She isn't our anything," I grit out. "And yes. She does."

"What's going on?" Declan notices we stopped and looks to see what we're staring at. I want to bury my face in my hands but settle for rolling my eyes. "Oh, hey. There's Shea and Violet. You guys want to go say hi?" Of course, by now, the entire group of girls—potentially the whole bar—have noticed we're here, so they're staring our way. He gives them a nod, and I'm pretty sure at least half of the group dissolves into giggles, waving.

Not Shea. Her gaze finds mine, and the smile that had been on her face a minute ago disappears.

I shake my head. "They're dancing. Let's go sit down. They see us. I'm sure they'll drop back." My words stop Declan, who already took a couple of steps in their direction. There's a question in the look he gives me, but I ignore it, heading instead for our seats. When I get there, I position a chair so I have a view of the dance floor and catch the first waitress I see to get a drink. I spend the next hour there.

Violet and a couple of her friends stop over. She hugs us all and tells us how excited she is to watch us play this year. Violet is from Texas, and she's a ball of sunshine. I'm glad she's sticking around, even though she and Nate broke up. She's friends with a lot of the puck bunnies, so I guess she sees the hockey team as part of her family, too, even though Nate was too much of an idiot to hold on to her.

Ash and Declan join the group on the dance floor first, and later, Griff makes his way out there. I stay put, though. I'm not great company, and as the night goes on, I watch Shea dance with guy after guy and laugh with the girls, and my mood deteriorates.

Ash returns, sliding his chair next to me, and downs the end of his bottle as he waves toward the waitress for another round. "You want one?" he asks.

"Sure." I polish off what remains in mine with a few gulps.

He holds up two fingers to the waitress and points at his empty bottle. She nods, hurrying off, and he sets down his empty. "What's up your ass tonight?"

"Nothing's up my ass." I say it in a growl, though, so we both know I'm lying.

"Really?" He lifts his eyebrows. "Because you're just sitting here, glaring at anyone who dances with Shea."

"No, I'm not," I say, even as I need to drop my gaze to stop doing exactly what he accused me of doing.

"What's up with you two, Reynolds?" He leans in, keeping his words between us. "You said that she's practically your sister, yet we all see the way you look at her." He shakes his head. "That's not a brotherly look."

"Fuck you, Draper."

"That's no explanation, dickhead."

"What does this matter to you?" I snarl at him.

He pauses and accepts the beers from the waitress. He sets the bottles down with an ominous thud. "If you're not willing to man up for her, then maybe I'd like to ask her to spend some time with me."

My fists tighten on the table, and I slam one down just hard enough to rattle the bottles and get the attention of a few of the people around us. I force my shoulders to relax and unclench my fists, stretching out my fingers. *Breathe, breathe...*

Next to me, Ash holds my gaze, and we stare at each other. He remains steady, completely self-assured, and though I've already come to respect the guy, the fact that he's not buckling under my irritation raises my estimation of him further.

That forces me to *really* look at him. Ash is a lot of the things that Shea deserves. He comes from money. His family owns a shipping company in Florida. If he doesn't make it into the NHL—which he might, if he's as good as he's looked in practice —he'll still have prospects. He's studying chemistry or something, one of the tougher majors, not some gimme major so he can play hockey. He's obviously smart. He's a considerate roommate, respectful to any of the girls I've seen him interact with, and he's got a quick wit.

If he checks so many boxes, and I like him so much, then why the hell do I want to rip his fucking throat out right now?

"You need to relax." Ash leans closer. "You feel that? There's nothing that gets rid of that, my man. That twisted ball inside your chest? The one that's angry and possessive and tied up with a bunch of grief?"

I meet his eyes, and there's something deep and weary there.

"That's what happens to assholes like us. It's regret. And if you don't do something about it, you'll live with that shit for the rest of your life." He stands up next to me and pats me on the shoulder. "I don't plan to mess with your girl. I have my own shit going on. I just wanted to get your attention. You're a great guy, Reynolds. Don't fuck this up."

"She's my best friend's sister, Ash." The words grind out of me, full of sorrow as I stare out at where she's dancing, having a good time. "How can I do this?"

"You love her, you dumbass. How can you not?" He leaves me alone at the table with that, heading toward the dance floor. I watch him shimmy through the crowd as if he didn't just throw a bomb at everything I thought I was doing.

I do love her. I've loved her for as long as I can remember.

Is he right? Am I fucking this up? My whole life, I've always done what I'm supposed to do. Dutiful son, loyal friend, reliable, trustworthy. I've prided myself on that shit, held onto it with two hands. It's always been clear what the right thing is, and most of that is not letting down the people I care about.

What Ash is suggesting? If I get any closer to Shea, it betrays Colt's trust. He'll never forgive me. Because I know that if I keep along this path, I'm going to touch her, and there's no going back from that. Either she'll agree, or she won't, but both options end Colt's faith in me.

But I can't be her friend any longer. Trying to pretend I can is impossible. It's too hard to be near her, wanting her like I do. When she was dating Justin, she wasn't around much. I watched over her when she was here, and it was easier to stay aloof, to pretend. I could tell myself I only wanted her because I couldn't have her. I'd sleep with other girls, and I'd pat myself on the back that I didn't have it that bad for Shea, that I wasn't that far gone.

I take a few gulps from my drink, watching them all dance. Declan and Griff are on the other side of the dance floor, having paired off with girls. They're dancing with them, whispering in their ears, putting on their moves. The sorority group has broken off into two factions. Ash shakes his ass with Violet and two of her other friends while Shea and the girl with red hair dance together, holding each other's hands.

Despite the confusion circling my head, I smile, watching her have fun. She's definitely had a few. The thought makes me chuckle. Shea cannot hold her booze. The telltale color is in her cheeks, and she's wobbling a bit on her heels as she waves her arms around, but she's still the most gorgeous thing I've ever seen, flamboyant dance moves and all.

As I watch, three guys shift their dancing positions to get closer to Shea and her dance partner. I recognize the one who steps behind Shea, dropping his hands on her hips and curving his huge body around her, as Roman Ellison, the quarterback for the Chesterboro University team. The two guys with him are Cameron Little, a running back, and Ryder Tate, one of the wide receivers.

My beer bottle hits the table with a thud, and I'm on my feet without realizing it. I watch as his hands curve around to rub against her jean-covered thighs. She tries to glance behind her to see who it is as he runs his hands up her hips to settle at her waist.

I've covered the distance between us by the time his hand slides under the hem of her tank top, and she stiffens.

Shea

I'VE BEEN DRINKING. I'M not ugly drunk, but I'm a few mixed drinks and a shot tipsy.

And I'm dancing. A lot. I love dancing. Justin hated dancing, so I rarely did it with him at State, and I've barely been at CU enough to go to parties or bars. But though drinking and I aren't really friends, dancing and me? We're tight.

I spend the night shaking my backside on the dance floor. I'm wearing my favorite jeans, the ones that make my butt look good. They've got a high waist and rips at the knees, and they look great with my gray booties. I put on a loose tank top because I assumed it was going to be hot on the dance floor, and I didn't want anything to make me uncomfortable. Tonight, I planned to dance and have fun and forget about Linc Reynolds.

Then he and the hockey boys showed up. I refuse to let them absorb my oxygen, though. He didn't even come over to say hello. I drown that sting with a shot.

I try to ignore him. I only look over to where he's sitting occasionally, and even then, it's quick.

He looks upset. The longer I dance, the more I wonder if something's wrong. Colt and I texted earlier about this.

Something's going on with Linc, but we can't figure it out. Colt says he's distant with him too.

I wonder if he's skating all right. I haven't asked him how he's been with the panic attacks. I should. It could be his family, his mom's MS. I hope everything's okay there.

Even as I worry, I feel stupid. He would tell me if he wanted me to know, and that's the whole problem. He doesn't want to tell me all that stuff. I'm only his best friend's sister.

That makes me mad, and I suck down another drink.

I make dancing friends with one of Violet's sisters, Penny. She's got red hair and a sly sense of humor, and she doesn't care if everyone looks at her. I guess when you're a redhead, it's hard to hide. But her energy makes me happy, and we dance, and I pretend that I can't feel Linc across the room.

I have to admit—I have a good time. Linc's roommates drop by and say hello. Then Penny and I start twirling around. That's when some huge guy steps up and starts grinding up against me. Penny stiffens and steps back, slipping into the crowd.

I'd give my new partner some liberty. We're dancing. Sometimes, guys put their hands on women when they dance. I'm wearing heels, and he could be trying to steady me. I've been drinking. But when his hand creeps under my tank top, I stiffen. Definitely not incidental contact.

I grip his wandering fingers and squeeze. I'm about to let him know what I think. That's when I glance up and find Linc in front of me. If I thought he looked upset before, he passed upset on the way over here and hit nuclear.

"Ellison." His voice is strong and leaves no room to be ignored. "Hands off."

The hands at my waist stop, and I turn. There's no room to move out here, so I find myself pressed between two gigantic guys—Linc and Roman Ellison, the quarterback for the Chesterboro football team. Even in my heels, I struggle to make eye contact. But they're doing a good job of staring each other down without me.

"Hey, Reynolds. How are you?" Roman's voice is even, and his stance remains loose, but the two other football players who step up beside him obviously sense danger. They don't smile. One of them is Teddy Little. I've heard he's a loose cannon.

"You've got your hands somewhere you shouldn't." Linc doesn't acknowledge Roman's friends.

I've hung out with guys my whole life. This is not a safe situation.

I place my hand on Linc's chest and try to make eye contact. He's not looking at me, though. "Linc," I say, trying to get his attention. "It's fine."

"It's not fine, Shea." His words are for me, but his eyes are only for Roman. I shift, getting my shoulders between them, and I put hands on both of their chests.

"This is unnecessary," I insist. Around us, other dancers step back. No one seems to know what's going on, but everyone can feel the tension in the air, and they clearly don't want to get involved. "I'm fine."

"Is there a problem here?" The extra room around us is suddenly full as Declan and Ash join us with two other guys from the hockey team that I don't know. Declan's got his arms folded over his chest.

This is going to get out of hand. "No," I say loudly, pushing harder between Roman and Linc, but it's like moving two mountains. They ignore me. "There's nothing wrong. Roman was dancing with me."

"Was he, now?" The words are a question, technically, but the way Declan says them is a threat. "Then why's he staring at my defenseman like that, Shea?"

"Oh, for crying out loud..." I mutter. Why did I think that Declan was going to be any help in this situation?

"What's going on?" Griff steps forward to join Declan. The music is still loud, but the whole place has stopped moving. Heat floods my face. We're making a scene. Griff nods at Roman. "Hey, Ellison. What's up?"

"Wondering why your guys are being rude, Parker." Roman finally glances away from Linc, cocking his head at Griff. "Any reason Reynolds would interrupt my dance with this lovely lady?"

Griff takes in all of us. I don't have that many interactions with him, but he's sharp. His face splits into a peacemaking grin. "Well, this lady is a good friend of his." He steps forward and throws an arm over Roman's shoulder. "Why don't you let me buy you a beer?" There's a pause as everyone stares each other down.

Finally, Roman's face folds into a lazy grin. "Sure, Griff. Sounds good." He must have decided that this wasn't worth a scuffle, not in the middle of the football season. I let out a sigh of relief and drop my hands.

The football guys follow Griff and Roman off the dance floor, but I've had enough. Nothing kills a buzz like male posturing. The rest of the crowd disperses. I glare up at Linc, whose face is closed off. "You acted like a caveman."

He shrugs, no hint of remorse on his face.

"I'm leaving."

I scan the crowd until I find Violet. While others have returned to dancing, she's studying Linc and me. I hug her.

"Call me tomorrow."

"Absolutely." Her gaze remains on Linc behind me, her brows high. I stick my tongue out at her. Her brows drop in concern. "You sure you can get home?"

No way I'm staying here another second. "It's a short walk. I have my phone."

She nods, still obviously worried. But I don't wait and push through the crowd, heading toward the door.

Vaguely, I hear Linc call my name behind me, but I don't stop. If I do, the things I say will make an even bigger scene, and I've been the center of attention enough already tonight.

The cool air hits my face once I'm outside. Fall has officially arrived in Chesterboro. There are people out here smoking, and I cut through the crowd. It's only a couple of blocks until I'm on campus proper, so I'm not too afraid to walk by myself, but I hustle anyway. I'm freezing in my tank top.

"Shea, slow down."

I don't want to talk to him right now.

I pick up my pace, but he's going to catch up with me—there's no way around it. His legs are longer than mine, so he covers the ground faster than me. Besides, in heels, I can only go so fast. I make the right onto Westover Street to cut through the alley behind the Convent. I wouldn't go this way alone, but Linc's right behind me, so I'm safe. He grabs my wrist, pulling me to a stop. "Shea, come on. Wait up."

"Let go." There isn't a lot of light here, only what's streaming from the streetlight. But at least we're alone. I tug my arm from his grasp and glare up at him. "I don't want to talk to you right now. If you want to walk me home, fine. But don't talk to me." I spin and head forward. I'm around the corner from my bed and the end of this disastrous evening.

"Shea, please stop." There is a hint of frustration in his voice, and whatever hold I have on my temper evaporates.

"No, Linc. You stop. That whole scene in there was embarrassing. What were you doing, anyway? The guy was dancing with me. I was about to tell him to watch his hands, and you broke in like some Neanderthal picking a fight." I replay the events in my head, and I'm even more mortified.

"That wasn't dancing. He was feeling you up." Linc scowls down at me, his hands on his hips, so I square off, mimicking his stance.

"He was handsy, not feeling me up." There was no boob action. None at all.

"Well, he shouldn't have been that handsy with you," he growls out.

"It's not your job to decide that. It's my job. And I was handling it." I wave my arms in exasperation. "Besides, there were a whole bunch of guys in that bar tonight getting handsy with a whole bunch of different girls. I didn't see you stepping in on their dancing." It's hard to be this close to him. Even though I'm angry with him, I'm still so aware of his bulk in front of me.

"Those girls aren't you. Jesus, Shea. I can't watch that stuff." He sounds irritated but something else too. Something wounded and even raw.

"What stuff?" I fold my arms around myself. Now that my anger is waning a bit, I'm cold again. I rub my arms.

"I can't watch someone touch you like that." His voice is soft and broken, and he steps closer. His hands fall on my shoulders, and he rubs up and down on the skin in the same warming movement I was doing a moment earlier. Except when he does it, it sends a different kind of heat coursing through me.

"Why, Linc?" I whisper. My heartbeat picks up as I meet his tortured gaze.

He opens his mouth, but no words come out. All he does is shake his head.

"Because you don't have to watch. Not really." I step out of his grasp and back away, needing to put space between us.

He said as much the other night. He might not like the thought of other people touching me, but he won't step over the line with me because of Colt. I get that—I really do. Linc's Colt's oldest friend—they're more like brothers, no matter how much I want him. Unable to continue looking at him, I duck my head, hug my arms tighter around myself, and do the fastest walk-run I've ever managed in heeled booties.

All I want is to escape to the privacy of my room and forget this entire night—Walter and his tears, the football player scene, and the way Linc Reynolds can continue to break my heart.

I'm about to turn the corner when he catches my arm again. I'm moving so quickly, though, that it upsets my balance, and I stumble backward. He steadies me easily, capturing me against him. Pressed against his chest, I can feel the hard, strong lines of him. He backs me up until we're leaning against the wall of my building, his forearms the only thing keeping me from the rough bricks. He buries his hands in my hair, and a gasp escapes my lips. He tilts my face up to his, leaning closer so we're staring at each other. I don't want to look away from the intensity in his green gaze, and I couldn't even if I tried, I'm so cradled in his embrace.

It should be overwhelming or even frightening to be held this completely by anyone, but all I feel is safe and desperate for him to touch me more, anywhere, however he wants.

He drops his face closer to mine until I can feel his warm breath on my cheek. I shiver, but I'm not cold any longer. Not at all.

"Damn it, Shea," he whispers in my ear. "I don't want anyone's hands on you but mine."

The words set me on fire, and I grip the back of his shirt in my hands, holding on. There's the softest rub of his mouth on my jaw, and I whimper.

"My God, you're gorgeous. Your skin, it's as soft as it looks." He runs his fingers along the back of my neck, and I tilt my head back, resting it against the wall behind him, exposing my neck to him. He runs his finger along my collarbone before I feel the warm swipe of his tongue on the sensitive skin beneath my ear.

It's the briefest rub, but it turns me on more than any other touch has in my entire life.

"Fuck, tiny girl... you are all I want in this whole world." He runs his thumbs along my jawbone, pulling back to gaze into my eyes. The emotion there is raw and intense, and it takes the breath out of my lungs. "Watching anyone else touch you is like knives in my stomach." He cups my face and presses a tender kiss to my forehead.

He treats me like I'm a piece of glass that might break if he handles it too roughly, but I want him to kiss me, to touch me, to consume me with whatever I see burning in his eyes. I know it with the kind of certainty that one knows the sky is blue and that fire will burn.

"What are you saying?" I whisper to him, my eyes searching his. My voice is breathless, achy. I press myself against him, stepping more fully between his legs, and I feel the hard press of him against my stomach.

Quickly, he takes two steps away from me, pulling his hands away from my face as if my touch hurt him. Without him, I'm immediately cold, and I drop my hands, bracing myself against the wall behind me, needing something solid to steady myself.

He paces a few steps in both directions like a caged lion before burying one of his hands in his hair. "It doesn't matter."

"What?" *It doesn't matter...* I wait for him to respond, to expand, to give me some explanation of what doesn't matter.

But he doesn't. He only closes his eyes and shakes his head at me. "It doesn't matter that I want to touch you. You're not for me."

I've felt rejection before. For four years, I dated a man I could never make happy. I know this feeling too well. "I see."

I do. He's right—it doesn't matter if I want him, because if he doesn't want me enough to take a chance on me, then there's nothing else for us.

If I were him, I'm not sure I'd take a chance on me either.

I push away from the wall and wrap my arms back around me, lifting my chin. "Please stay away from me, Linc. You're right. This is too hard."

Shea

BETWEEN THE ALCOHOL AND what happened with Linc, I can't sleep. I toss and turn all night. I have weird dreams and lots of anxiety, and I finally give up at six. I sip Gatorade and nurse my head on the couch, watching reruns of some reality dating show until I can text Violet at a reasonable hour.

She texts right back. *Americano?*

You're a goddess.

I am. See you in fifteen.

I buzz her up fourteen minutes later.

She breezes into my room with her face free of makeup and her blond hair in a bun. She's beauty-queen perfect. I've never seen Violet look anything less than beautiful. She rolls out of bed that way, I think. It would be annoying if I didn't like her so much.

"Morning, sunshine," she sings, handing me my drink. I take it and blow her a kiss.

"Ugh," I reply. "I hate drinking." I sip my Americano, sighing. Coffee makes everything better.

"We all do... until the next time." She plops down on the couch next to me. "So," she starts, dragging the word out, "you and Linc Reynolds. Spill it, sister."

"There is no Linc and me. He told me I wasn't for him. And he's my brother's best friend, so he doesn't want to mess everything up, but I'm afraid everything is all messed up anyway." I spill that all in one breath.

"Whoa." She lowers her takeaway cup, her eyes wide. "You're going to have to start at the beginning, I think."

I do. I've never breathed a word about my crush on Linc, but I tell Violet all about it. I tell her about how things shifted when I started dating Justin and how Linc kept his distance those years. I tell her about the gala and how he said he'd help me find a date, but I haven't been able to think about anyone but him since then. I pretty much spew out every confusing thing I've felt about him in one jumble of rambling until I don't have anything else I can say, and I fall silent.

"Wow." She blinks. "When I thought you might have a rebound this year, I definitely didn't expect this."

"He's not a rebound," I insist.

She raises her eyebrows at me.

"No, seriously. Linc has nothing to do with Justin."

"Really? Because that's what all girls who just broke up with someone say when they rebound." She shrugs. "At least that was what I said after Nate." A flash of pain clouds her eyes, but it's gone so quickly that I can't be sure it was there at all. She's been struggling with their breakup. She doesn't talk about it much, but when she does, I see how it's hurting her.

I shake my head. "I feel like I started getting over Justin months before we broke up. I can't even believe I stayed with him so long." As I say the words, I realize how true they are. I stash that away, determined to think it through further at some point.

"You're a loyal one, Carmichael. You stayed with him because you like to make people happy." She states it like a fact.

I shift in my seat, suddenly uncomfortable. "Everyone likes to make people happy."

"I know, but you would rather make other people happy than focus on what makes you happy." She puts her cup on the coffee table. "Like this thing with Linc."

I wrap my blanket tighter around myself. "I don't see what this has to do with Linc."

"Well, what are you going to do about him?" She asks, folding her hands in her lap.

"What can I do?" I throw up my hands. "He doesn't want to mess everything up."

"You said it's already messed up." She lifts her eyebrows.

"It is," I exclaim. "And he's fine with it being messed up."

"Is he?" She pauses, cocking her head. "Well, then, are you?"

"Am I what?" I'm confused.

"Happy with things between you two being messed up."

I consider. Am I okay with the state of things, this current status quo? I shake my head. "No."

This isn't fine with me. I don't know when things changed with Linc. In the years I dated Justin, I pretended the crush I had on Linc was the result of him being nice to me. But I can be stubborn. It was what kept me with Justin and made me keep trying when I should have let things go. Those years, I would never have let myself even consider that I had real, meaningful feelings for Linc.

God, I was stupid. Steadfast and devoted but also stupid, placing my loyalty in Justin when it was so obvious that he didn't deserve it. Now, without that baggage, everything looks different.

Violet leans forward and places her hand on my knee. She's so rarely serious, usually the picture of happy thoughts and sunny conversation, that it's strange to see the depth of emotion on her face. Offhand, I wonder exactly how much she hides. "What is it that you want, Shea?"

"I want him." I can't keep the words in any longer. I don't want to, but I *do* want him. I don't know if it'll work, and I don't know if I should, but that doesn't change how I feel.

Her gaze is sympathetic. "Did you tell him that?"

"No." I snort. Like she needs to ask. She knows me better than that.

"Why not?" she asks gently. "If you want him, why didn't you say so?" She squeezes my leg.

Violet's more intuitive than I ever give her credit for. "Because he keeps saying that I'm his best friend's sister and that none of the stuff he feels matters."

"I'm not talking about him. I'm talking about you. What you feel matters." She emphasizes the last word, and I let it sink into my bones.

She's right—I matter. I might not understand all of this. Okay, I definitely don't understand it, but that's not the point. I want him. I'm sure of it, and I'm almost as sure that he wants me too.

"You should tell him, babe. Tell him that you want him. Put it all out there. Say the words." She shakes her head, sadness creeping into her expression again. "We don't have infinite time. If you want something, you should ask for it." Her face firms, the sadness gone, replaced by something stronger. "He might not agree. It might not work. Hell, it might be embarrassing. But are you going to leave everything to some 'mights' and chances?"

I shake my head. "I don't know, Vi..." That sounds great. Worthy of a motivational poster. But that's not who I've ever been before.

"You are a badass, Shea Carmichael," she says, taking my hands. "You don't know it yet, but everyone else does. And you deserve to ask for what you need. You might not get it. Trust me, that happens. But at least then, you've asked. You'll know the answer. But you won't know the answer unless you ask." She waves a graceful hand. "What's the worst that can happen? He says no? Isn't it already a no?"

I nod. It's true—the way things are now is a solid "no."

"Well, then, sometimes you need to stand up for what you deserve. If you want this guy, then you need to tell him." She nods decisively, like it's all settled. She picks up her coffee, drains it, and drops it in the trash. "You know what you need right now?"

I don't, so I only shake my head.

"Greasy breakfast. Get up. We're going to the truck stop." The truck stop near the interstate has the best homestyle food around.

"Sold. But you drive." I drank too much. My head still hurts.

"Sounds good. Let's go."

I laugh and head into my bedroom to find some sneakers. My hair's a hot mess, so I grab a hair tie and pull it up into a bun. As I stare into the mirror, fixing my hair, I decide that Violet is right—I do deserve to ask for what I want. But how does someone actually do that? Do I call him, out of the blue, and tell him that I want him?

I chuckle because I can't even imagine how that would play out. My grin fades, and I sigh. I have no idea where things go from here. I do know, though, that from now on, I'm going to take my friend's advice.

I need to take control of my own happiness. From here on out, I'm done being the girl who always puts herself last. I'm going to voice my wants and needs. I nod at myself before rolling my eyes. Well, at least I'm going to give it a shot.

Linc

"REYNOLDS. YOU DECENT?" DECLAN'S voice breaks into my crazy dreams.

I have no idea what time it is, but there's light streaming in the window. I roll over and cover my head with my pillow. "No."

"Great." The door swings open. I clutch the pillow tighter around my head.

"I'm sleeping, dickhead."

"No, you aren't. Besides, it's almost noon. We have practice after lunch."

"Fuck." I roll onto my back and cover my face. My head aches, probably from a mixture of one too many beers and too much Shea Carmichael on my mind. I squeeze my eyes closed, but I can't shake the memory of her, staring up at me in the moonlight, her lips soft and pink.

"Well, you shouldn't have been drinking like a freshman last night," Declan says, cutting into my stupid mental images. I pull the pillow away so I can give him the finger. He gives me a wave from where he leans against the door frame. "Besides, I need to talk to you."

I sigh. I guess I'm done tossing and turning for today. Swinging my legs over the side of my bed, I bury my head in my hands, trying to stop its pounding. "What's up?" I ask, rubbing my eyes and gazing up at him.

He closes the door. Damn it, that's not a good sign. Then he drops into my desk chair and studies me, his brows low. "You look like shit."

"Thanks?" I offer.

"No, for real, Linc. What's going on with you?"

"What do you mean?" I stand up, searching the room for a T-shirt or something to throw on. This doesn't seem like the kind of conversation I want to have in my boxers.

"What the hell happened last night?" I find a pair of basketball shorts and a Chesterboro Bulldogs hockey T-shirt. I shrug into them instead of answering, so Declan continues. "You almost got us into a fight in the middle of Fat Eddie's. We need to talk about that."

"No one got into a fight, Mitch. I was only talking to Ellison." I cross my arms over my chest.

"Because Griff jumped in and defused the situation." He glares at me. "I know you. You had your I'm-a-second-from-kicking-your-ass face on. I've seen it before. But we were right in the middle of a bar, right before the season starts. You can't pull that shit. We don't need that kind of publicity."

"Ellison didn't need bad press either," I mutter. It's a lame deflection, and I know it.

He narrows his eyes. "Is that really your fucking excuse?"

He's right—I could have gotten all of us into trouble last night. I'm not usually a hothead like that. "You're right. I was out of line."

"You were," he says, but a lot of the anger has bled out of his expression. "What the hell, though? There are guys on the team that I expect to act like meatheads, but you're not one of them."

"Shea..." I say her name, but I don't even know where I'm going with it.

"I'm sure that Shea didn't want you to get in a fight over her," Declan offers.

"Of course not." As far as I could tell, she was mortified that I drew that much attention to her in the first place. I exhale heavily. "But Ellison..."

"She's not your girl, Linc. They were dancing." He pauses. "If he'd hurt her, I'd have your back in a heartbeat, and you wouldn't be getting this shit from me. But he didn't. She was handling it."

"I know. I just..." The explanation gets caught in my throat.

"She's not yours." He emphasizes the words. He stands and buries his hands in his pockets. "You can't take those kinds of risks. Not with yourself and not with the team. Whatever is going on with you and her, you need to figure it out. Soon." He leaves, pulling the door closed behind him.

I bury my hands in my hair, staring after him. I can't refute anything he said, and that hitches up my frustration. I used to tell myself I had this under control. It's obvious that I don't.

I'm not sure what almost happened between Shea and me last night, but it's inexcusable. It would have changed things with Colt, and if I had thrown hands with Ellison, it would have caused a huge headache for my team.

Nothing has changed with Shea. She's still not for me. Forgetting that is only going to get me into trouble.

Linc

A WEEK AFTER I almost kissed Shea in a dark and dirty alley, her brother calls me while I'm lifting in the weight room. I've spent the past seven days working out as hard as I can so that when I fall into bed at night, I won't dream of Shea.

It's not working. I can't stop thinking about her. No matter how tired I am, no matter how much my muscles ache, she's in my mind all the time.

I let Colt's call go to voicemail. The weight room is loud, full of guys and music. I finish my reps then snag my phone. In the hall outside, I call him back. "Hey. What's up?"

"Where have you been, Reynolds?" he demands.

Fine, I have been avoiding his texts. Most of the time, Colt and I chat in fits and starts all week. We go over the latest hockey news. He tells me about things in Philadelphia. It sounds like a cool city. I tell him about school, studiously leaving any mention of Shea out. He doesn't seem to notice, only asking me about hockey and how things are going on the ice. The answer is good. I really think our team has a chance this year. Last year, we made it to the final round and suffered a heartbreaking loss. I'm hoping this year will be different.

"I'm training. Why you stalking me, Carmichael?" I fire back, even though I have to force down a flare of guilt. I haven't reached out, and I know it, but it's harder and harder to pretend things are normal when things are so jacked up with Shea.

"I need a favor."

"Yeah?" I'm immediately wary. Colt wouldn't ask for something lightly.

"I can't go to the gala, the one that my mom and Peterson's mother are responsible for organizing. Do you know what I'm talking about?"

I do, but because I don't say anything right away, he goes on.

"It's the one that my family hosts. I told Shea that I would be going because I'm in town. But our PR rep scheduled me for another fundraiser, and I can't get out of it."

"That sucks," I say into the pause.

"Yeah. But she planned to go by herself. I figured I'd be there to hang out with her. My parents won't have a chance to keep her company. They're always busy at these things. So if I don't go, she's going to be alone."

"I thought she planned to get a date." She's been on dates. Guys notice her. I'm inappropriately aware of all that attention. Why isn't she taking someone?

"Me too. Apparently not. She's been sending lots of girl-power-ish texts. She told me some long thing about how she's taking care of herself or something." He snorts. "I don't think she realized how personal that sounded. But I can't let her deal with Peterson by herself."

"So you want me—"

"Take my ticket. Go in my place. The thing is already paid for. It costs some ridiculous amount of money, so I'm sure the food is going to be good. Just go and keep her company."

"Colt..." I exhale. "I don't think she wants me to go." Before he can ask me why, I hurry on. "If she did, she would have asked me herself, wouldn't she?"

"I know you're busy, buddy, and I know that the season is about to start. But it's Shea. We can't let her go there by herself. Peterson and his fiancée will be there." I can almost picture him pacing and worrying. "I feel bad. I told her I'd be there. I don't want to let her down. Please. You know I wouldn't ask if it wasn't important. Help me out."

"Okay." The word damns me even as a part of me I wish I could ignore is already thrilled about the prospect of being with Shea. It's out of line. Since the night outside her apartment, I've stayed away from her, and she's done the same. It's been a week, and I don't know what to say. There's nothing more to say. She told me to leave her alone. "She's going to be pissed at you." That probably doesn't cover it. She's going to be livid. "She's going to be mad at both of us."

"Maybe. But she can't stay mad at me for long." I can hear the grin in his voice.

"I don't know, Colt..."

"I'll have a tux sent to your room at the hotel. It's under my name." He gives me the name of a hotel. "I'll cover your train into the city. I'll take care of everything."

"Fine. But you need to tell her that you aren't going to be there and that you're sending me instead."

"Fine. I'll tell her." He promises to text me all the details, and we hang up.

Damn it. I should have put up a bigger fight. She's going to be disappointed that Colt won't be there, but she doesn't want me there at all.

Except I'm already excited that I'll get to be there with her, to see her and spend time with her. When it comes to Shea, I'll take whatever I can get.

I bury my hands in my hair. I'm trying not to fuck everything up, but trying to keep things the same is fucked up already. I slam my palm against the cinderblock wall, and then I go back into the weight room. After my reps, I need a nice, long, painful run.

Shea

I SPEND MOST OF the afternoon before the Food Bank Gala primping with my mother. We get massages then go to my mother's favorite salon for manicures and pedicures.

It's fun to hang out with her. I didn't see her much this summer. She and Dad had a lot of things going on in the city, so she was only in the Hamptons a few weekends. My internship kept me busy and on Long Island, or I would have driven in to see her. It's nice to have this time to catch up.

Except she keeps asking me if I've been dating, if there's anyone interesting. She doesn't come right out and say the exact words, but she thinks it's strange I didn't get a date to the gala. I don't think my mother has ever attended a function without a date.

I doubt she gave Colt this kind of trouble. She never bugs him about his love life, even though there are pictures of him with different girls at different events all the time. Then again, maybe she does nag him, and that's why he can't make it tonight.

I tell her that I'll be fine at the gala alone. I'm sure I'll know more than a few people there. I've been going to this thing since I was in high school.

I get dressed at the penthouse then ride with my parents to the hotel. The driver helps me get my overnight bag out of the trunk. When Colt canceled, I figured I'd take the room we'd booked to share. I could take a car back to the penthouse later, but I plan to have a few drinks, so I don't feel like riding in a car. Besides, if I stay here at the hotel, I can sleep in and get breakfast in the morning, maybe even squeeze in another massage before I have to head back to Chesterboro. Classes have been kicking my butt so far this semester, and a five-star hotel bed and room service sound like exactly what the doctor ordered.

I promise my parents I'll meet them in the ballroom after I drop off my bag. I stop at the registration desk, and the man behind the desk hands me a key card. "Welcome, Miss Carmichael. The other member of your party has already checked in."

My brow drops. "I'm sorry. You're mistaken." Colt was supposed to share the suite with me. It's got two bedrooms. But he told me he wasn't going to be here.

"Colton Carmichael. Is he not on your registration?" I can see the man's anxiety hitch up. I'm sure that the clientele who rent the high-end suites on the top few floors don't appreciate snafus. I wave it off, not wanting to stress him out.

"He is. You know what? I'm sure it's no problem." Maybe Colt's plans changed. He told me he had a fundraiser and was trying to get out of it. I head for the elevator bank. As I ride up, I smile, my spirits lifting. If Colt's here, this whole event just got a whole lot more fun.

I hurry down the hallway to locate my room, swipe my key card, then push inside. "Colt, you're here..." Except the words die on my lips. It's not Colt standing shirtless in the middle of the suite. It's Linc.

His back is to me, but I'm sure it's him even without seeing his face. I'd know his body anywhere. As he turns, his expression unreadable, my breath hitches. My God, how can he be more attractive every time I see him? I would have sworn it was physically impossible, but here he stands. He's been working hard, training and skating. At least that's what I've gathered when I've risked asking our mutual friends how things are going. That's what one does when they're staunchly avoiding someone—they creep on them through other people.

We stand there, staring at each other, me in my evening gown and the cashmere pashmina I threw over it to stave off the cold air, and him shirtless, in tuxedo pants and with bare feet.

Linc Reynolds has the hottest feet in the world. "You're not Colt," I offer dumbly.

"No." He picks up the tuxedo shirt he'd been reaching for when I walked in and throws it on, leaving it unbuttoned. "He told you he wasn't coming, right?"

"Yes. But he didn't tell me you were." I roll my bag inside and close the door behind me. "I thought the room would be empty and that I could stay here tonight."

"Wait. He told me that he was going to tell you that he gave me his ticket." His eyes storm over. "So you didn't know that I was going to be here?"

I shake my head. He puts his hands on his waist. "I'm so sorry, Shea." He sounds legitimately apologetic. "He told me that I should take the room when he asked me to take his ticket. He said you'd be staying with your parents."

I shrug off my shawl, using that as an excuse to turn away from him. As I fold it, I close my eyes, bracing myself. *God damn it, Colt.* Why didn't he tell me? Except I know why. He knows I would tell him not to send Linc and that I don't need a chaperon, and that would have caused an argument. Overbearing jerk that he is, he took the choice away from me. I'm surrounded by men who think it's their job to take care of me all the time.

"I'm going to kill him," I mumble, but as I face Linc, I forget how pissed I am.

The look on his face... it's part wonder and part fire, and it sets waves of awareness along my spine. He's staring at my dress, at me, and he swallows. "You look so beautiful."

It's such a genuine compliment, and it fills me with pleasure. "Thank you. My mother picked out the dress." I hadn't had time to go shopping, but I couldn't have picked anything prettier. Mom has impeccable taste. The design isn't elaborate, but it's perfectly cut and in a deep emerald with spaghetti straps and a deep V in the front. The fabric is alternating satin and chiffon, and the panels twirl around me as I walk.

He shakes his head. "It's not the dress, Shea. It's definitely you."

It's an honest confession, and I'm filled with the familiar mix of confusion and fire that seems to always be inside me when Linc is here. I duck my head, heat on my cheeks. "You shouldn't say things like that to me." *Because I love to hear them too much...*

"Probably not. But it's the truth."

"Linc..." I shake my head. "When you say things like that to me, it makes me think you might be interested... that you could..." I can't get the words out. For all my desire to take charge of what I want, it's a lot harder than it sounds. I remember him saying that I'm like a sister to him as clearly as if it were yesterday. He's so loyal to my brother. How do I say that I want him in a way that overcomes those things?

"Let's go to this party, Shea." He takes my hand, stepping closer. He smells like him—the amazing cologne he wears and that warm thing that's all him. His shirt is still unbuttoned, and I'm insanely aware of the planes of his chest. I gaze up at his face, and his eyes are raw. "We're both here. Let's just go and have a good time." When I don't immediately agree, he smiles. "You didn't want to go by yourself, did you?"

I shake my head. Of course not. Who wants to go stag to an event with a bunch of couples?

"I know that you're not thrilled about it, but I can be your date." He squeezes my hand, my fingers entirely engulfed in his warm grip. "I want to be your date."

I ignore all my doubts. He might be here because of my brother or because he didn't want me to be alone. He could even be here because he hates how things have been so strange between us.

Right now, I only want to be with him, even if he isn't here for the reasons I wish he was. For tonight, I'm going to enjoy his company and pretend that there can somehow be a chance for us.

Linc

AFTER I FINISH GETTING dressed, Shea helps me with my bow tie. Then she goes into the bathroom to freshen up or whatever girls do, and I text her brother.

Me: *What the fuck, Colt? Why didn't you tell Shea I was coming?*

Colt: *She would have told me not to send you. But she needs a friend.*

Me: *We need to talk about what a controlling asshole you are sometimes.*

Colt: *Whatever. Tell her hey for me and that I'll talk to her tomorrow.*

I pocket my phone. I can't bitch at him too much. I want to be here with her, even though I shouldn't. Who's the asshole now? She comes out of the bathroom, and again, I'm struck mute by how absolutely beautiful she looks. That dress is something else, but I wasn't lying before—it's not the dress. It's the girl in it. Shea always manages to leave me breathless.

I offer her my arm to steady her on her heels, and we head down to the ballroom. I can't help but stand tall with her beside me.

The gala is one of the fanciest dinners I've ever attended. We sit with Shea's parents, who seem genuinely excited to see me. There are two other couples there too. The Cornwalls are an older couple. Mr. Cornwall is the head of a hedge fund and an economic think tank. The other couple is a senator from Connecticut and her husband.

A few tables away, Shea's ex, Justin Peterson, is sitting with his parents and the girl he brought to the Carmichaels' summer party, his fiancée. Shea and I both ignore him, but I can feel his eyes on us.

Look all you want, asshole. You fucked up. Shea isn't mine, but I'm glad she's not with him anymore.

Shea is as gracious with the high-powered personalities at our table as she is with my hockey guys over for pizza at her place. What could be an awkward situation, a grouping of people who just met, is smoothed over by her and her mother. They ask good questions and are curious about everyone. There's laughter and interesting conversations. We chat about politics without arguing—a huge feat in itself—and Shea mediates when her father and the hedge fund manager get too heated about business dealings. It's clear that she's managing everything and everyone, but she's so genuine about it. I truly feel like none of the table guests want to upset her, so they go along with it.

Dessert and coffee are served, and she laughs when she sees the plate. How does her laugh make me happy and hard at the same time?

"Cannoli," Shea says with a sigh. "Thank goodness."

Mrs. Cornwall next to her tilts her head in question.

Shea waves her fork before scooping up a heap of ricotta filling. "Sometimes, these events have fussy desserts. But I think that dessert is best when it's straightforward, unassuming, and plain delicious."

"Hold on. Straightforward? Unassuming? You baked cookies with applesauce instead of oil," I remind her. "That was not straightforward."

Mrs. Cornwall tsks at her. "Oh, my dear. That's a sin."

I smother a laugh with my napkin as Shea puffs up. "I baked those for Linc and his roommates who all play competitive hockey and are very concerned about their physical fitness and well-being. I was trying to be healthy. And eggs are high in cholesterol."

Mrs. Cornwall looks me over. "Miss Carmichael, it's obvious this man does not need to watch his cholesterol. He's quite clearly in amazing condition."

My ears feel hot as Shea covers a giggle. I nod to the older woman. "Why thank you, Mrs. Cornwall. I appreciate that."

"You're welcome, dear," she responds, digging into her dessert and sighing. "Oh, it is wonderful, isn't it?"

"Martha, are you flirting with Shea's date?" her husband scolds.

Mrs. Cornwall waves him off, fully committed to her cannoli. "Only a little, love. He's being very kind about it."

Shea rolls her eyes. "Don't let him charm you, Mrs. Cornwall. One second he's sweet, but the next thing you know, he's insulting your baked goods."

Mrs. Cornwall laughs. Her husband grins, shakes his head, and stands. "Come, Martha. I believe the dance floor is calling our name."

She leaves her dessert and smiles up at her husband, her eyes soft on him. "You're right, Arthur." She takes his hand, and the two of them head off.

Next to me, Shea sighs, tucking her elbow on the table, a wistful look on her face as she watches them.

"What?" I ask.

"The Cornwalls have been married since right out of high school. They're from a small town in central New Jersey. He commuted back and forth to New York as they got their start, and she quit working when they had kids so he could travel for his job. Then she went back to work to help him pay for graduate school. They had a lot of ups and downs, but they're so clearly still in love." She picks up her fork and digs back in to the last few bites of her dessert. "I want that."

"You want to struggle financially?" I wrinkle my nose. "Trust me, my family struggles financially sometimes, and it's not that much fun."

"No, that's not it. I mean, they have had each other's back. That's all." She sips her coffee, obviously uncomfortable.

I use the moment when her attention is diverted to look at her. The lights are low, and the table is covered in candlelight. Her long hair is arranged in a whole mass of curls on top of her hair, and her lips are the creamiest red. And that dress... Christ, whoever designed that number, with its hints of cleavage and soft swirling fabric, is definitely into torture, because it's been driving me wild all night. I've barely managed to not stare at her chest like a stupid middle-schooler.

She deserves someone to have her back like she says. She deserves the very best, not to have to struggle, to always feel loved and cared for.

I've watched my parents stress over money my whole life. It hasn't been easy for them. There's nothing romantic about being strapped for cash.

Do I really think that things will be different for me? I'm barely hanging on to the funds to go to college. My place on the hockey team is less than secure—one more concussion, and I'll be out. I have no idea what will happen with my hockey career. Right now, I feel good on the ice, but making it in the NHL is competitive, rigorous. I got drafted, but I haven't signed any contracts yet, and none are guaranteed for me.

I have no idea what my future holds. How the hell could I ever think it would be good enough for her?

"Come and dance with me?" I ask, desperate to ignore all my doubts for now. Tonight, all I want is to enjoy her company.

She finishes chewing, pats her mouth with her napkin, then sets it aside. Her eyes meet mine, shining in the candlelight, and I hold my hand out for her. Together, we head to the dance floor. Across the room, I see Justin watching us, his face sour. But this isn't about him. It's about Shea, me, and this one night when I'm purposely forgetting that she's not mine.

On the dance floor, I slide one hand behind her back and pull her against me. I tuck her other hand in mine and start us around the floor.

Before my mother's MS got really bad, she used to love to dance. Not wiggle-your-ass kind of dancing but actual dances, the box step and the waltz. I'm naturally athletic, so I picked things up pretty easily. We would twirl around our living room any chance she got.

Right now, I slide Shea into a waltz, and we glide along.

"You know how to dance." She's surprised, and it makes me smile. We've known each other so long, I'm happy I can still set her off balance.

"I'm not completely uncultured." She's beyond gorgeous this evening and feels like heaven in my arms. Usually, when I hold her, it's because of a quick hug or some other brief contact. Every time, I've been aware that I shouldn't crave her touch like I do. I brace myself against the contact. But here, she's in my arms, and it's acceptable, in front of all these people, to hold her, to look at her without guarding everything. I'm sure everyone can see that I think she's beautiful. Hell, they'd need to be blind not to see it themselves. But on this dance floor, it's appropriate, and I bask in the sheer freedom of looking at her without guilt.

"You're not uncultured at all." She gazes up at me, a soft smile on her face. "I mean, I don't know how to dance. Not like this. You're leading me, and I'm just following you. Actually, you're practically carrying me."

She's right, but it's easy enough to cover her minor missteps. "I'll carry you anywhere."

She glances up quickly, meeting my eyes. Confusion flickers there, and I hate that things are like this with us. I've tangled everything up, and it's as if I can't stop myself anymore. "I'm sorry."

"Why?" She asks, her gaze fixing on my forehead. It gives me a moment to stare at her mouth.

"Because you're Colt's sister. I shouldn't say that stuff—hell, I shouldn't feel that stuff at all." All of that is true, but none of it is going to stop me. I don't think there's a way to stop it now.

We keep dancing, and she searches my face, her eyes troubled. God, I want to kiss her, right here. I don't care who's around. I want to pull her closer, to take those full lips, stained red tonight, in my mouth. I want to breathe her breath and taste her mouth.

"What do you feel?" she asks.

I close my eyes and shake my head. I've done this. I've dragged us this close to the line we shouldn't cross. I'm an asshole, and I'm ruining everything.

The music stops, and we stop dancing. I meet her eyes then, and she stays in the circle of my embrace, her hands clutching my arms. I can feel a shiver move through her, and I drop my hands to her waist. She's so slight in my arms.

"Because you aren't the only one, Linc. I want you to say that stuff, to call me beautiful, to touch me." Her voice breaks, but she swallows and keeps going. "I want you. You have to know that by now."

I can only stare at her, at her beautiful face, full of earnestness.

"I know it's going to be complicated. I know you're my brother's friend. But I want you, and I don't think you only think I'm beautiful." She lets out a shaky breath. "I think that you want me too."

Something inside me breaks, sweeping away whatever holds the last of my restraint. "Shea..." My fingers press into the silky fabric of her dress. My throat tightens, trapping all the words I want to say. This is going to change everything. There's no coming back from this. It's both a relief and an agony. I swallow. "My God. I can't..." *I can't stay away from you any longer. I don't want to, not when you say things like that.*

She stiffens and steps back, something painful on her face. "Right. Of course. You can't. I'm... please, excuse me." She glances away, her eyes bouncing around the room. "I'm going to the ladies' room."

"Wait. Shea, hold on."

She steps away, heading toward the lobby, leaving me standing there in the middle of the dance floor. My God. What happened? *I can't...*

Oh shit. I hurry after her.

Shea

I PUSH THROUGH A door to leave the ballroom and suck in a handful of breaths that don't seem to deliver any oxygen to my brain.

Oh my God, did I just do that? Did I confess that to him and implode everything? When Violet suggested that I tell him how I felt, that not knowing couldn't be any worse than the answer, I don't think I properly dwelt on how hard a "no" would hit me. Now that I've said the words, I can't unsay them. We can't go back. Hanging in limbo would have been better than this.

I set off toward the restroom, my heels clicking purposely on the marble as my embarrassment gives way to anger. I didn't read things wrong. I'm sure he's attracted to me. He said so. He's holding back because of Colt, because whatever bro code they have keeps him from doing anything about it.

I only need a few minutes to get myself together, and then I'll be able to go back in there and scrounge up whatever's left of my pride. I might even tell Linc Reynolds exactly how stupid I think he's being.

Maybe.

Justin steps through a side door from the ballroom. He must have figured out I was going to the ladies' room and planned to cut me off. I exhale. Besides Linc, Justin is the last person I want to see in this moment.

"Shea," he greets me, and I stop. He's between the restroom and me, and the hallway isn't that wide.

There's no polite way around him. I consider being impolite and promptly disregard it. My mother would die if she found out I was rude to him. "Hello, Justin." I don't think I could sound less happy to see him.

"Hi." He runs a hand over his hair. The nervous motion is unlike him. He's usually perfectly composed. "You look breathtaking."

"Thank you." I manage a sick smile. "If you'll excuse me, I'm on my way to the restroom." I move to skirt around him now that I've managed a social greeting, but he grabs my arm.

"Shea, please. All I need is a second." I stare at where he's holding my arm, and he drops his grasp. "I wanted to tell you that... that you and Reynolds make a really good-looking couple."

I snort a laugh. I can't help myself—after what just happened, that strikes me as hysterical. "Oh, we're not a couple." I have no idea what's become of our relationship or friendship or whatever we have, but I'm sure of at least that much.

He shakes his head. "It's just... the way you look at him."

I put my hands on my hips, not even caring how it looks right now. I scowl at him. "How exactly do I look at him, Justin?"

"Like he's some kind of hero. I don't know that you ever looked at me like that."

I don't know if he means it to sound accusing, but my nerves are raw. I spent enough time feeling like he was finding flaws with me. I don't need to listen to this anymore. We aren't together. I open my mouth to say so, but I'm interrupted.

"She didn't look at you like that because you're a selfish prick." Linc offers from behind us. I close my eyes, praying for patience.

"Linc, stay out of this," I say.

Linc shrugs. He's got his hands tucked into his tuxedo pants, his jacket hanging over one elbow.

I hate how good-looking he is, because I don't want to find him attractive when I'm this irritated with him.

"You took her for granted. She deserves better than that."

I glare at him. "Now you know what I do and don't deserve?" I raise my eyebrows.

He flinches. "Shea..."

I hold up my hand. "Stop."

I spin to Justin, catching him by surprise. "You," I say, pointing at him. "Who I look at isn't your concern. You got engaged a few months after our breakup. Which, by the way, is extremely tasteless. Therefore, you don't get to judge me at all."

I wave a hand, dismissing him, and scowl at Linc. "And you." I narrow my eyes. "You are the most overbearing, confusing, frustrating person I've ever met."

The two of them stand there, blinking at me. I throw up my hands at them. "If you'll excuse me"—I smooth out my gown and take a steadying breath—"I've had enough fun for tonight." I nod to Justin. "You should get back to your fiancée. And you," I say to Linc. "I'll see you back at school."

Justin narrows his eyes at Linc, but he does as he's told with his head up. I huff out a breath as I head to the elevators then hit the button, wrapping my arms around myself.

This night started perfectly. Linc looks movie-star handsome in a tux, and he's the most attentive date. We got to sit with the Cornwalls, whom I adore. Then they gave us cannoli for dessert.

But dancing with Linc was the highlight. It wasn't only that his body was perfect, all muscle and control, though that was definitely nice. No, it was the way he held me, as if I was the most precious thing in the world. Justin noticed how I looked at him, but I was too busy looking at the way Linc watched me.

Linc joins me to wait for the elevator, and we stand there in silence. Finally, I say, "I told you that I want to be left alone."

"No, you didn't," he clarifies. "You said you had enough of the party for tonight. So have I."

"I meant that I've had enough of you," I snap at him, immediately regretting being mean. I've never been the kind of girl who can be nasty easily. I always feel immediate remorse. "Sorry. That's not—"

"Shea, stop." He grins. "I get it. I'm overbearing, confusing, and frustrating. You said that already." He chuckles, staring at the numbers as they light up, indicating the elevator's descent.

I want to stomp my foot at him, but that would be childish. Instead, I swipe a strand of hair out of my eyes and sniff. "Well, you are."

"You're right." He hands me my clutch bag. "I stopped back at the table to get this for you." He shrugs a shoulder. "I assumed we were done there for the night."

I'm still figuring out what that means as the elevator door opens, and I step inside and turn toward the door. He follows me in, standing directly in front of me. The door closes, and he reaches beside him and pulls the lever to keep the door shut.

I cock my head. "What are you...?" But my words die as he moves closer, cups my face in his hands, and buries his fingertips in the hair at the nape of my neck. He surrounds me, and I can't breathe, only stare up at him.

His eyes search mine. "You didn't stay in the ballroom long enough to let me finish." His voice is soft, low, and full of emotion.

"Finish what?" I swallow, because with his hands on me, I struggle to form coherent sentences. I cup his elbows to steady myself as I drown in his eyes.

"You are exactly right, tiny girl. I do want you. I feel like I've always wanted you. I want you so damn much that it's all I think about all the time. I used to be able to keep it in check, but I can't. Not anymore." He drops his forehead to mine and whispers, "I can't stay away from you, Shea. I don't want to."

The words send waves of aching heat through me. I grip his arms tighter, unsteady on my feet.

"Fuck, I want to kiss you so badly. Please?"

I nod. "Yes." The word is barely out when his lips crash down on mine.

His mouth is perfect. The pressure, the moisture... everything about him against me with his hands in my hair feels exactly like it's supposed to be this way. I press closer to him, gripping the back of his tuxedo jacket. Vaguely, I hear my clutch hit the floor. I don't care.

We kiss until I can't tell where one kiss ends and the next starts. I never want him to stop, not ever, and I fold myself against him, shaking with need, wanting to get my hands on his skin.

He pulls back, as breathless as I am. He holds my face still and drops a few more kisses on my lips. "We can't do this here," he mutters as he shifts away. He presses the lever to get the elevator going again, rubbing my arm. "Are you cold?"

I shake my head. "Not even a little."

"You're shivering," he says as he shifts out of his jacket and wraps it over around my shoulders, pulling me closer.

"Not because I'm cold," I respond, gazing up at him again. He rubs his thumb over my lower lip, and then he does it again. His head drops, and he drags the same lip between his teeth, sucking on it, and I'm afraid I might melt into the elevator floor. A vague ding causes Linc to raise his head.

"Sorry," he says over his shoulder. I can't see who he's talking to, though, because his bulk obscures my view. "We're going up." He presses the door close button repeatedly until it slides closed, and I dissolve into giggles.

Moments later, we arrive at our floor, and the door slides open too slowly. He hustles me down the hall toward the room. When I'm not fast enough, thanks to my obscenely high heels, he sweeps me into his arms and carries me the rest of the way to the door with long strides.

Standing me up, he makes sure I'm steady before he swipes his key. Then we're inside, and the door swings closed behind us.

In the middle of the suite's foyer, he drops his key card onto the table next to the door and puts his hands on my shoulders. As always, he's gentle, almost reverent. Not as if I'm fragile but like I'm priceless. It's arousing and humbling all at once.

His eyes are hot on me. My breathing is heavier than it should be, and I can hardly hear around my heartbeat. We're here, in this hotel room, together. Anticipation laces through my stomach, mixing with the arousal already settled there.

"Shea," he begins, running his hands over his hair. He's tense. I have no idea what words are about to come out of his mouth, but if they're second thoughts, I don't want them.

"Linc, let's not have that talk," I plead, because I'm sure that if we start talking about this, it'll break whatever spell we're under. "Tonight doesn't have anything to do with anyone but us. I want you, Linc, and you want me. For tonight, let's just let that be enough."

Something uncertain flashes across his face, but then he nods. "Tonight."

I exhale.

He doesn't break his eye contact as he unbuttons his cuffs then pulls his tie apart and unbuttons the top button.

Linc

THIS IS A MISTAKE. Unforgivable.

I ignore that internal voice, because this is Shea. It doesn't feel like a mistake—it feels perfect. I've wanted her for so long, I can barely remember a time when I didn't.

I reach for her and help her out of my tuxedo jacket. To be fair, she looks better in it than I did. I run my hands over her uncovered shoulders, reveling in the softness of her. She closes her eyes, breathing out my name on an uneven breath. The sound settles in my groin. I didn't think it was possible to be harder than I was before, but apparently, I was wrong.

I cup her face again and recapture her mouth with mine. My God, there's nothing that tastes better than her. She's addictive. There was a time, when I was younger and dumber, that I thought if I could only kiss her—one time—that it would be enough, and I'd be able to get her out of my head. But that's not true. There's nothing about this that quenches anything.

I move my lips over hers, and she sways, so I catch her against me. It gives me the chance to change the angle of our mouths, and I sweep my tongue through hers, inhaling her gasp.

When I can finally lift my lips from hers, I find the zipper at the back of her dress. With a slow slide, I tug it down, and the dress falls into a pool of fabric on the floor.

She looked stunning in the dress, but nothing prepares me for the sight of her in an emerald lace corset and those strappy gold heels.

"Holy fuck," I growl out. "That corset..."

She smooths her hands over it as a flush covers her cheeks and creeps across her chest. "Do you like it?"

"That's the hottest fucking thing I've ever seen." There's so much gravel in my throat, my voice sounds garbled.

Still blushing, she offers me the slightest shrug. "I really love pretty lingerie."

I trace a finger across the lace that lines the top of the corset along her breastbone, and her breath hitches. "Tiny, I also really love your pretty lingerie."

She reaches over her head and starts pulling the pins out of her hair. I step behind her and help, but I get distracted by the soft strands. She drops her hands, letting me take over for her. I gently untangle each pin from her hair, sweeping my fingers through the long strands until they fall around her shoulders in waves. From this angle, I stare down the front of her, and lust like I've never felt before surges through me. I'm no monk. But this is different. This girl is different. She always has been.

I sweep her hair to one side and drop my mouth to the sensitive skin at the base of her neck. I rain kisses along her collarbone, inhaling the scent of her, lavender, and something citrus. I place open-mouthed kisses there, and she tilts her head to the side, giving me more access as she leans back against me. I move my hands from where they were cupping her shoulders, down the length of her arms, and then up across the raspy lace of her corset.

I wasn't lying—the fucking thing is right out of my teenage wet dreams. As I cup her breasts through the lace, she arches into my hands, and I swear I might go off in my pants at the sight of her straining into my touch.

I close my eyes for a moment, sucking in a deep breath, desperate to hold my shit together. I've wanted her so long, there's no way I'm going to ruin it now. When I finally have a grip on my galloping lust, I gently pull the lace covering her breasts down.

Shea's petite in all ways. She's not tall—she has a small bone structure, and her breasts are the same. They fit perfectly in my hands, the nipples hard and tight against my palms. I rub them with my thumb. She gasps, and her knees buckle, sending her weight fully against me. I can easily manage it. She reaches a hand up, tangling it in my hair, and the feeling of her fingers at the nape of my neck is heaven.

I need more, though.

She's already leaning against me, so it's easy to catch her up into my arms. As she gazes up at me, her pupils are dilated, and her lips are pink, well-kissed. She's the sexiest woman I've ever seen.

This hotel room is huge, especially considering that it's in the middle of Manhattan. There's the common area that we came into, then two bedrooms off of that, each with its own bathroom. I pick the closest bedroom.

There aren't any lights on, but I can see from the light in the other room. I fling the bedspread off the king bed and lay Shea in the middle of it, turning on the lamp next to the bed. With her dark hair splayed around her, her heels still on, and that fucking corset she's wearing pulled down beneath her breasts, she's a fucking goddess. Except the color is high on her cheeks, and she won't meet my eyes.

Concern lances through me, and everything stops. I sit down next to her as she shifts to sit on the bed, pulling the lace back up and over her breasts. "Whoa." I reach for her hand and squeeze her fingers. "I was looking at that." I wink at her, but her flush only deepens, and she still isn't holding my eye contact. "Hey," I say to her. "Are you okay?"

She glances at the light. "Do you think, maybe, we could... I don't know, turn that off?" She sits, reaching for her heels. Her posture screams discomfort, and I'm instantly tense.

I scoot closer to her, capturing her hands. "Hey." I wait, not moving. This isn't right. I have no idea what's going on, but somewhere between the common room and the bed, something changed. I shush her, and she stills. Her gaze meets mine, filled with uncertainty. I hate it. "What happened?"

She shrugs, waving at the nightstand. "The light and... I don't know."

"Do you want to stop?" If she says yes, we will, even if it's the hardest thing I do.

"No." She shakes her head. "Absolutely not."

"Okay. Good. That's good." My relief is so intense, it's almost physical. "So talk to me."

"It's just... I'm practically naked."

"I definitely noticed." I can't help but grin, letting my eyes roam over her. "Deliciously so."

Her flush deepens. "And you're..." She waves me over.

I'm still not sure what she's talking about. "I'm not naked?" I offer. She blinks at me. "Well, that's easy enough to fix."

I kick off my dress shoes as I get to work on the rest of the buttons on my shirt. Shea watches, and if I'm not mistaken, she looks less uncomfortable with each button. That gets me moving faster. I pull the shirt off, and her eyes are definitely focused on me now. The heat I see in her expression amps me up, and I reach for my belt. "Are we doing any better?" I mean it to sound light, but my voice is raspy.

She nods, her eyes still fixed on my chest. I tug on the belt buckle, but my hands aren't as steady with her gaze on me like that. I manage to unbutton and unzip, drop my pants and boxers to the ground, and step out of them. I motion to my feet. I'm still wearing my dress socks. "Socks or no socks, my lady?"

She giggles. "No socks, Reynolds. Your feet are hot." Whatever discomfort she'd been struggling with before is gone.

I wink at her. "That's definitely not a compliment I've heard before."

She shrugs, still grinning. "It's true." But her smile fades as I tug them off and fling them across the room. "Jesus, Linc." She sighs, and her eyes are wide. "You're wonderful."

I'm not shy, and I don't lack confidence. I'm athletic, and I work out a lot. If the reflection in the mirror doesn't convince me that my body is in top shape, the way that women look at me does. But I never really let that get to my head. The girl I always wanted didn't seem to notice me, so it's hard to get too cocky.

But now, she sees me. The combination of her eyes on me and the way she said those words fills me with the strangest possessive tenderness I've ever felt. No matter how many girls have told me they liked what they saw, only Shea matters.

I sit next to her and motion to her feet. "Mind if we lose these heels? They make your legs look hot, but they seem sharp." I offer her a grin, still trying to keep things light.

She nods, and I tackle the minuscule buckles at her ankles. They're so small, though, that my fingers struggle. Or I'm wound so tightly, not wanting to scare her off, that I can't keep my hands from shaking. "Jesus, woman. How do you even walk in these things?"

She leans forward to help, smiling. "Very carefully." I leave her to the straps and instead watch her breasts sway under the lace of her corset. Her nipples are the prettiest color—not pink, exactly, but the darkest, dustiest rose.

Finally, she drops her heels over the side of the bed. It's been entirely too long since I touched her, so I shift, sitting cross-legged, and reach for her. She comes into my arms willingly, and I position her, straddling my lap, facing me. I push her hair off her shoulders and take in the shape of her corset. There's a line of hooks down the front of it. I might not know my way around sandal straps, but these are pretty straightforward bra hooks. These, I can manage.

With a handful of flicks, I unlatch the thing into two sides, leaving them apart at her waist. Her chest rises and falls quickly as I duck down and capture one of her exquisite nipples in my mouth. Her sigh is the stuff of dreams. I suck the hard tip in my mouth, pulling her deep, and she arches into me, gripping my shoulders. Her touch feels so good that I need to struggle to keep my eyes open to make sure I see her. I refuse to miss a moment of my time with her.

I repeat the caress on the other side, glancing up at her. Her head is tilted back, her lips open, and she's magnificent. Cradling her in my arms, I lean her back on the bedsheets. Her hair drops in a waterfall around her, and her eyes are glazed.

"I need to taste you," I murmur. I reach for the corset then shimmy it down her legs and toss it over the bed with the rest of our clothes. Positioned here, between her legs, I can see every inch of her. "You are truly the most beautiful woman I've ever seen."

The flush returns to her cheeks, but she pants, and I can't wait any longer. I rearrange my bulk so that I'm lying between her knees. I tuck my arms under her thighs. She's completely bare and freshly waxed, and I swear, I'm glad I'm lying on my dick right now. The discomfort of it wedged underneath me keeps me from making a fool of myself. "Shea?" I glance up the length of her body.

Her fingers grip the sheets next to her, her knuckles white. "Yes?" She breathes out.

"I'm going to go down on you now." I wait, giving her a moment to stop me. *Please, whatever gods control the universe, please don't let her stop me...*

"Oh yes..." The last word comes out on a moan, and I groan as I part the folds at the center of her and run my tongue from her opening to her clit in one long, flat sweep.

She bucks, crying out. "Linc... that's... oh my God..."

That's a pretty nice-sounding word salad, so I do it again, and then I fall into a slow, steady rhythm against her warm, soft skin. Shea's mouth might taste like heaven, but the taste of her here is sinful. The feel of her against my tongue and my lips... She's soaking wet, and I can't get enough of it.

She moves against my mouth, and I hold her steady, increasing my tempo and pressure the slightest bit until she's muttering nonsense. A whole lot of my name and God's name, all mashed together. I watch her, and the sight of her like this sends electricity down my spine. I'm close to coming just from licking her off.

The prettiest flush covers her chest, and her color is high. I move so I can bury two fingers in her wet opening, and she explodes on my hand. Shudders run through her body and the soft center of her grips my fingers. The noises she makes are the hottest, sexiest things I've ever heard in my life. I continue to work her through the orgasm, licking more gently as she comes down.

I press a last kiss against her soft folds before crawling up her body and gathering her against me. I cradle her, listen to her breathing, and feel her heartbeat against my chest. I've never been more content in my entire life.

This girl is it for me.

Shea

LINC HOLDS ME AS I gather myself. My back is against his front, and he's still rock hard, pressing into my spine. But he doesn't appear in any rush to hurry me along. He's so much taller than me that he creates a cocoon around me, and the fingers of his right hand run lazy circles on the skin on my shoulder and arm. His strong heart beats erratically against my back.

"Linc?" I ask because I need to break the silence.

"Yeah?"

I roll so I can see his face. "Thank you."

His brows crease, and he cocks his head.

"For that. That was... I mean, that was, really incredible." I close my eyes, feeling stupid. *God, I sound like a moron.* Justin didn't really like to talk about sex things, so I'm not comfortable saying much about it either.

"Shea, please. I should be thanking you. That was the hottest thing I've ever watched." He chuckles.

"Well, I mean, not every guy likes to, you know, do that." As soon as the words leave my mouth, I'm mortified. "You know..."

"No, Tiny." The furrow in his brow deepens. "I don't know." He studies me, and I bite my lip. "Shea, Justin went down on you, right?"

He looks so grouchy that I shrug and try to wave him off. "I mean, sure. A few times. He just, well, he said that it got messy."

"If you're doing it right, yeah." Now Linc's stiff, and his outrage is palpable.

I continue as if he didn't speak. "So sometimes he didn't want to," I finish. I'm playing it down. Justin might have gone down on me a handful of times. But after he complained, I stopped asking.

"Did you give him blow jobs?"

My cheeks burst into flames. "Of course. Guys like blow jobs." I smile, but it feels sickly.

Linc pulls me into his arms, tucking my head under his chin, running his fingers along my back. One thing I've noticed about him is that he's constantly touching, stroking, and rubbing me, as if he can't get enough of the feel of my skin. He mutters a bunch of stuff about Justin under his breath, but none of it is kind. One thing catches my attention.

"What did you say about him?" I ask, adjusting myself to stare up into his fierce green eyes. Though this is kind of embarrassing, it's also sweet to see him so frustrated on my behalf. I knew that Justin could be selfish, but after the orgasm Linc gave me, it hits a new level.

"I said that of course he's a fucking sixty-eight." He grunts. When I cock my head in question, he adds, "He can't be a sixty-nine, because he always owes you one."

I crack up, and his irritation leaves his face, replaced by a sheepish grin. I press against his chest, coaxing him onto his back. He had his chance to touch—and I'm definitely not complaining—but now, it's my turn.

He accommodates me. Earlier, I was nervous. Justin didn't like to have sex with the lights on, same as he didn't like to talk about sexual things or go down on me. In fact, Justin had a lot of rules about a lot of things. It was no wonder I constantly worried that I was going to disappoint him.

But I don't think there's a thing I can do right now that Linc won't like. That's a heady realization, and it emboldens me. Right now, he sprawls on his back, his hands tucked behind his head, in all his Greek-god glory. I mean, Linc is impressive in clothes, but without them, he's extraordinary.

I look him over, and when my eyes return to his, he waggles his eyebrows at me. "What do you think, huh? Pretty good, right?"

He's right, obviously. But I tap my finger against my lips. "You know, I think I'd like a closer look."

He spreads his arms out. "Have whatever you like, sweetheart."

I believe him. He's relaxed with a lazy smile, so much different than the tense Linc who has been treating me with kid gloves the past few months. But his eyes are clear and open, and there's nothing I want more than to touch him.

I throw my leg over his waist to straddle him, wiping the grin right off his face. What replaces it is all heat, and it ratchets me up in a way I never would have expected. I seat myself on his lower stomach and run my hands along his shoulders and down his chest.

There's nothing teasing or lighthearted in the way he looks at me now.

I lean forward and press my mouth on him. His skin is warm, and the muscles underneath quiver under my mouth. I breathe deeply then run my tongue along his sternum, needing to fill all my senses with him. His heartbeat is rapid beneath my fingers, and I can feel the hard length of him against my bottom, but I don't want to hurry. I run my hands along him, learning the angles and planes of his body. He's not cocky now, only staring down at me with fire. His fingers dig into my hips, his grip firm, and I relish it. Seeing him this way, when he's usually the picture of control... it's got me ready for him.

I shimmy down, allowing the still-wet core of me to rub against him, and he sucks in a desperate breath. "Jesus, Shea... I'm dying here."

"Hush," I whisper as I take the hard length of him in my hand. He comes off the bed, and I still, waiting for him to settle.

"Please..." He whispers, his voice raspy and deep, his eyes vulnerable.

I hold his gaze as I take him in my mouth.

"Oh, fuck..." He sighs, and that seems like a good sign, so I continue to work him over.

I'm finding my rhythm, when he rears back, picks me up, and tosses me on the bed next to him. "Hey," I complain.

"Shea, please... I need..." His voice is desperate, and I can't tease him, not when he's like this.

I smile up at him and cup his cheek in my hand. "Condom."

He nods. He's gone and back to me so fast, I barely have a chance to miss his warmth. He tears it open, but when his hands are shaking too much, I help him roll it on.

Poised over me, he runs his thumb over my lips. We're sweaty and disheveled, but everything about it is perfect. I don't care about the light anymore. I don't care that he's a hockey-playing god. We're only Shea and Linc, two people who have known each other forever. He's been my rock, the one I've counted on to steady me for years. When he pushes inside of me, it feels like I've come home.

He pauses, buried deep inside me. I grip his shoulder, shifting to accommodate the size of him. Nothing about him is small.

Concern tightens his face. "Are you okay?"

I run my fingers along his back, over his chest, and he closes his eyes on a groan. "I'm wonderful."

He cups my face with his hands, then he slides out and back in, and I'm lost. He tilts back to rest on his knees and drags me closer. The adjustment in position hits a spot inside me that makes me close my eyes and cry out. He sets us a slow rhythm, and I'm swimming in sensations. "Shea. Look at me."

I do as he asks, and the intensity in his eyes takes my breath away. "I want you to see us."

I glance down the expanse of our bodies, and nothing has ever made more sense to me than the way this feels and looks. Having Linc inside me fills all the blanks I've ever had and answers questions I didn't even know I was asking.

When I make eye contact again, I open my mouth, but no words come out, and then he picks up his pace, and any desire to talk escapes my brain. Instead, all I can do is watch him as he watches me, falling deeper into the feel of him as we move together. I can feel another orgasm racing forward, and as if he knows exactly what's happening, he reaches between our bodies and rubs my clit, sending me over the edge.

I cry his name and grip his arms as I ride out the waves of it, completely at its mercy. Linc continues moving, faster now, then shouts out his own release. I open my eyes in time to see bliss on his face, and nothing has ever been more beautiful to me.

When it's over, he snuggles up next to me and pulls me into his arms. I doze off, not wanting this night to end.

Linc

I WAKE IN THE early hours and reach for Shea. I don't want to spend a single moment of this night with any space between us. As I press her naked body against me, though, the friction wakes up my dick, and there's no way I can sleep. I try to stay still so I don't wake her, but her skin is so soft, and I drag my fingers along the base of her spine. She arches into me, and I go completely hard. Her fingers search me out, pulling my face down to hers.

What's next is frantic, almost desperate. I'm all straining muscles, reaching fingers, and open kisses. I never want to stop touching her, but we said this was only for tonight. If that's true, I need to memorize every inch of her, brand the taste of her in my mind.

When we're done, we fall apart, panting, and I stare up at the ceiling in the darkness, still holding her hand.

"Linc?"

"Yeah?" I'm afraid of whatever she's going to say.

"I know we said tonight, but..." She pauses, and I can hear her swallow. "I don't see why we can't keep going."

I frown at the ceiling, glad that the darkness hides my reaction. What she's suggesting is everything I want, but the hope that sings through me that this might not be over is completely wrong.

She hurries on when I don't say anything. "I mean, we aren't hurting anyone. And if you don't want to tell anyone, we don't need to."

"You want to be fuck buddies?" If considering her in a casual sexual relationship with anyone else bothered me before, thinking about us like that is worse. I don't want to be casual with her. Correction—nothing about the way I feel about her is casual and never has been.

I can feel her scowl, even in the dark. If I wasn't wrangling with all my stupid emotions, I might think it was funny. "No. I want to be friends but with benefits, I guess."

"Oh, well, then. That's much more civilized sounding." Why am I being this snappish with her? I'm angry at myself, not her.

"Fine. Forget about it." She swings her legs over the bed. As she's about to stand, though, I dive across the bed and grab her hand, pressing my mouth against it.

"I'm sorry." I gaze up at her, and there's not much light in here, but I can see the wariness on her face, and I hate it. "I'm an asshole." When she doesn't say anything immediately, I grovel. "Shea, I'm sorry. I didn't mean it."

"What did you mean, then?" She scowls at me and inhales a steadying breath. "Because I'm telling you that I want to do this more, that I want to spend more time with you. That I don't want this to last only for one night. And even if you need time to keep it to ourselves, I'm okay with that. So, what exactly are you telling me?"

I join her as we sit on the side of the bed, still holding her hand. Running my other hand through my hair, I tug on it, happy to feel the bite on my scalp, wishing that it could bring me some solution to this that isn't going to end in disaster.

Because I want that all, too, everything she said. I want her in my arms, in my bed, and next to me all the time. But I also want to be the friend to her brother that I always thought I was.

I promised him that I'd take care of her. That I'd help her find someone good for her, someone that would treat her right. Someone worthy of her.

What she's proposing doesn't check any of those boxes. My life is in chaos, I'm about to agree to be her secret fuck buddy, and there's no way that lying to her brother makes me worthy of her. Not even a bit.

But I *am* going to agree. When it comes to Shea, I'm weak. "I don't want this to be over either, Tiny."

"Then why does it have to be?"

I exhale. All the reasons rest on my lips, but I can't spit them out. "It doesn't." The words damn me, but if I can have Shea like this, even for a while, it's better than not having her at all. I'll deal with the consequences later.

She smiles up at me, but it's a sad smile, and I hate it. "You sound so excited."

She's right—if I'm all in on this, I need to hold these regrets down deep. I don't need to let all my bullshit rub off on her. "Oh, I'm definitely excited." I reach for her, dragging her onto my lap, then rain kisses down on her face and shoulders. My dick hardens. Christ, I'll never get used to the effect she has on me. "Still think I'm not excited?"

She giggles, swatting my hands away. "Hold on. I need to go to the bathroom."

I sweep her into my arms and head for the gigantic en suite. "You know what? I need to use that bathroom too. That bathtub looks like it might even be big enough for a six-four giant."

She laughs.

Shea

IT SURPRISES ME HOW easily Linc and I fall into our new arrangement.

This year, we've spent more time trying to avoid each other than anything else, so it's freeing to have that weight gone. I sit with the hockey guys most days at lunch unless schoolwork or study meetings interfere. If any of them think my presence is strange, they keep it to themselves. Violet joins me, but she keeps my secret like a champ. When she found out that Linc came to the gala, there was no way I could keep my relationship from her. I don't want to.

Either our friends have always assumed that Linc and I were secretly together, or we are a lot better at pretending nothing's going on between us than we thought we were. I'm not complaining—not having to explain myself makes everything much easier.

I wonder how Linc is explaining why he hasn't been sleeping at home the last three nights, though.

The one kink in all my happiness is Colt. We text constantly, and though he doesn't ask me outright if I'm sleeping with Linc—because why would he?— I don't offer the information, either. Lying by omission is still lying.

I told Linc that we could give it some time. It hasn't been a week yet, but I am already sure about how this feels. Being with him makes me happy. We aren't a normal couple who just met and are learning about each other. We have the benefit of having known each other forever. I spent four years with someone that I shouldn't have been with, knowing something wasn't quite right. But this feels right to me, and I want to tell everyone about it.

In the end, I'm sure Linc will come around, even if it means having a difficult conversation with my brother.

Linc stops over after practice on Wednesday night. He drops a bag of food onto the counter in my kitchenette then folds his arms around me where I'm sitting at my drafting table. I swat at him when his kisses become distracting. "Stop it. I need to finish this."

"What is that?" He asks, pulling the stool I keep in the kitchen next to me and studying the plans that are scattered across the desk. I want to curl into his body, but I hold myself together. I'm working.

"It's the next Habitat for Humanity project. After we worked on the last one, the director asked if I'd like to help design the next project." I show him a picture of a house here in Chesterboro. It's sadly run down and dated. The landscaping is overgrown and neglected.

I slide over the mockup I made for the new front. I added a porch and an additional bedroom and bathroom as a second floor. "The house is for a family of four, an immigrant couple and their two children. They're currently living in a one-bedroom apartment in the center of town. This home was only two-bedroom, one bath, straight out of the Depression era, so I added another bedroom and bathroom upstairs. But the backyard…" I riffle through the mess on my desk to find the rest of the pictures they sent me. "This backyard is exactly what two growing kids need." The lot is a quarter of an acre right at the edge of town. It's graded flat, too, so there's plenty of room for games of tag and kickball back there. "I even designed this to go in there." I show him the specs I drew of a playset. "I always wanted one of these as a child." My dad never wanted to add a playground on the back of any of our houses. For obvious reasons in New York—no yard at the penthouse—but he said they were an eyesore, and he didn't want one at the house in the Hamptons.

Linc studies everything, shifting the drawings and pictures around so he can take it all in. "These are wonderful. I like what you did to gable the back of the bathroom. This addition doesn't even look like it's out of place. It blends into the rest of the house's architecture flawlessly."

I raise my eyebrows, but I'm not sure why I'm surprised. He's helped his father on job sites for years. He knows his way around plans and specs. "Thanks. I'm excited about it."

"When does construction begin?" he asks.

"Not until after Thanksgiving." I bite my lip. "I really hope that there's enough time to finish it before the holidays. It would be nice to give this family a home at Christmas." That's why I've been rushing through these plans on top of my regular school work. It's one thing to do assignments for hypothetical homes or buildings, but it's entirely another to do work that directly benefits two children's lives.

"Let me know when you start. I'll bring the boys along again."

"You guys don't have to do that. You'll be in the middle of the season."

He kisses my cheek. "If we can come, we will." He winks at me. "Besides, you know you like to see me all sweaty and working construction. I'm hot."

"I mean, how will we get anything done, though? No room in a house this size with your ego." I point to the picture. "Not much square footage."

He grumbles and sweeps me up into his arms. Laughing, I play-slap at him. "Put me down, you jerk. I have work to do." But I don't really mean it, and he knows it. He hurries me into my bedroom and drops me on the bed. I laugh as he tickles me, but the giggles stop when he lifts my shirt and starts kissing my belly.

What follows is slow and sweet. We both take our time, touching and tasting each other. When it's over, I curl into his side and run my fingers along his chest.

"You really love doing rehab projects, don't you?" he asks.

I twist up to look at him, considering. "I do. I don't like wasting things. Too often, people want to tear things down instead of fixing them. Throw things away instead of repurposing them. I don't like the way that feels. Most of the time, you can take a house that has good bones and make it into what you need, if you only spend some time working with what you have and use some creativity. Not everything is meant to be easy."

"Sometimes there's more money in tearing down and starting from scratch," he points out. "Easier that way."

"Trust me, I know. I grew up with my father, remember?" I laugh, and it ends on a sigh. "But I don't want to only design the latest, most modern or technologically advanced projects. I like the challenge of giving something new life. A new purpose."

"How does that fit in at Carmichael Enterprises?"

We both shift onto our sides. I tuck my hands under my head, and he rests his head on his elbow, gazing down at me. I should feel awkward. We're naked, twisted up in the sheets. My entire chest is exposed, and I think his butt's hanging out. But I don't feel weird at all. Mostly, I feel safe in his company, like whatever I say here stays in the space between us. It's a heady feeling.

"I'm not going to work for Carmichael Enterprises." It's the first time I've said the words out loud. I've been coming to the realization for months, but now that I've let the decision out of my head, it feels real. Weighty. "I haven't told my father yet, but I don't want to do corporate design."

"Your dad would probably give you any position in the company that you wanted, corporate design or otherwise," Linc points out.

"Yes, but that's not really fair, is it?" I wrinkle my nose. "I can't pretend that I'm not extremely lucky or that things were hard for me. Because I know better than anyone exactly how much I've been given in my life. But it doesn't feel right for me to step in and take a job—a job I don't even really want to do—from someone who's worked to be there. Who *wants* to be there."

"Some would say the fact that you even have the choice to turn down the job is privileged."

If anyone but Linc had said that, I would think they were chastising me. "It is. And six months ago, I wouldn't have considered not taking the job. I wouldn't have considered defying my parents." I give a shrug. "But things are different now. I need to do what I want."

He tucks a strand of hair behind my ear. "And what is it that you want?"

"I'm not sure." I consider. "The woman I worked for this summer wants to talk to me when I get back to town. She does historic preservation and renovations on Long Island. I loved the work. I'm not sure that's what I want to do yet, but it's a lot closer to what I want than the corporate designs my dad's going to expect."

"Well, then you should do what makes you happy."

He sounds so matter-of-fact, as if there's no other choice. I laugh. "Have you met my father? He doesn't take no for an answer. That's why he's a wealthy billionaire businessman. It's literally his brand to be a hardass."

Linc kisses me on the forehead. "Yeah, but you're his daughter, not some company negotiation. You're his soft spot. It'll be different." He shifts. "I'm starving. I brought Chinese." He snags his boxers off the floor and struggles into them, barely pausing on his way back to the kitchen. He glances back at me with a wink. "I got you lo mein."

I watch him go. I disagree with him. I don't think my father's going to be fine if I don't work for him. It's been assumed my entire life that I'd step in to Carmichael Enterprises. Not in an executive position but as part of the creative team. In some ways, I get the feeling that my interest in design amuses my hard-nosed-businessman father, almost like my mother's charity work amuses him. He sees both ventures as important, but not as vital as the serious negotiations and business decisions he makes.

To some extent, that's always bothered me. I love to design, but it's not only about the art. I was drawn to architecture because it gives me the opportunity to improve upon reality, to create something better out of what is.

I'll need to let Dad know what I'm going to do, sooner than later. Knowing him, he's already settled me into a role in his corporation. I don't want to let planning for my arrival get too far. But if I'm serious about starting to take charge of my own decisions, to follow my own dreams and not only try to make everyone else happy, then I need to start accepting that I'm going to make some people unhappy. Even my parents.

Linc

THE FRIDAY AFTER THE gala is my first game. I'm a jittery bag of nerves. I barely slept this week. It's becoming more difficult to keep all this anxiety from Shea, but I don't want to upset her. I hope after this game is under my belt, everything will get easier.

The game is at home, against a rival from across the state. They're not in our division, so it doesn't count in the playoff standings, but even though the points won't count, the game is still important. It's my first time back on the ice in a competitive situation.

Everyone manages their stress differently. Declan needs to talk to everyone. He makes his rounds in the locker room, checking in, pumping everyone up like he's a fucking politician or something. Griff listens to music. I have no idea what's on his playlist, but he bobs his head along, tapping his fingers on whatever is around.

Ash looks sick. I'm pretty sure he's going to throw up.

I can't get too tangled up in their rituals, because I'm trying hard not to lose my shit. I haven't had a panic attack in a couple of months, but I can feel it resting in my chest, waiting.

I've never been a talker before a game, so when Declan stops by, I only shake my head at him. He nods and holds out his fist. I bump it with mine, and he moves on.

By the time we get called to the ice and the crowd goes wild, I'm sweating full-on, and my hands are shaking.

I glance up at the team section, where Shea's sitting in my seat. She's cheering, and when she sees me looking, she waves. I wave my stick at her, and her presence there steadies me. I drop my spare stick on the bench and do a few warmup laps around my goalie to stretch out my legs.

At puck drop, I'm itching to go. Coach has paired me with Griff on defense. It's probably a good match. I'm more of a true blueliner, staying on the point on offense. Griff is one of our tough guys with the kind of reputation that makes other teams think twice before running any of our offensive players. Griff's got an edge about him. It helps that he's taller than everyone on the team except me, but that's not it entirely. He's got a hint of violence in him. It's always contained. Even in the one fight he got into last season, he didn't lose control. He stepped up, pummeled his opponent, and skated off the rink for his automatic game disqualification. To me, he feels more dangerous because of that ironclad control. I'd hate to ever truly see him lose his shit.

But his defensive style compliments mine. While I'm more traditional and cautious in my play, he's more explosive. He never hesitates to skate low, if needed. Still, though he might be more unpredictable on the blue line, I've got the slap shot from up high that other teams need to adjust their strategy for.

I'm antsy on my first shift and can't settle down. But when I hit the ice on my second shift, I find my groove.

Everything is fine. Better than fine, actually. I throw my weight around like only a six-four guy can and manage to get off a slap shot that sets up a goal. I'm credited for two assists.

We beat them, 5-2. The locker room is fired up afterward, excited about our win. For me, this feels like more than a team triumph—it's a personal victory too.

I did it. I got out there and I played my ass off, and I helped my team get a win.

By the time I leave the locker room, I'm practically floating. Shea's waiting in the hall outside. She throws herself into my arms. "You did great!"

I twirl her around, laughing. I want to kiss her so badly right now, but there are too many people, so I force myself to set her on her feet. I use her heeled boots as an excuse to touch her for a few extra moments. Really, though, I only want to hold her.

"How do you feel?" she asks, still grinning up at me.

"Great. Never better." I'm not lying either. For the first time in a long time, I let myself wonder if everything might actually be okay. I played great, better than ever. With play like that, the Gladiators will have to recognize me, and a contract in the near future will solve all my problems. My college expenses, my mom's medical bills, everything.

It's amazing what financial security could fix.

She squeezes my hand. I get the impression that she wants to touch more of me, too, but she doesn't. Instead, her gaze follows one of the sophomores and his girlfriend. I don't know the girl, but she's swimming in the guy's away jersey. All the girls wear their guys' away jerseys to the home games. It's a badge of honor among the bunnies.

Her expression drops the slightest bit. She's talked about our future relationship with ease a few times this week. She's called me her boyfriend, and I love that. She's ready to tell everyone. She wants to tell Colt.

The way I played tonight gives me hope that I might be able to get a handle on the chaos in my life. I don't like lying to Colt either. I talk to the guy almost every day. He asks how things are. He asks about Shea. I hate pretending that things are still the same when they aren't.

They're better. I'm happier with her than I've ever been. I need to figure out the right way and the right time to tell him.

All those things are clogging up my head, and I don't want them to. I want to ride the high from our win and take Shea home to bed. I open my mouth to suggest we go back to her place when Declan comes out of the locker room and interrupts me.

"Party's at Shepherd, Reynolds. Get your ass there."

"I was about to..." Damn it, I don't want to go to a party right now. I want to take Shea home and have our own celebration.

"You wear the A, pal. You need to be there."

I curse again, but he's right. The team presented me and Griff with assistant captain letters yesterday. I'm touched, but I forgot that I'd probably need to be more involved as a leader, and that includes being around to wrangle the young guys after their first win.

"Sorry, Shea. I have to go to this party." I shrug helplessly.

She scans my face, and the smile she offers is too bright. "Right. Of course. I'll just... um, go back home. I'll talk to you tomorrow." She steps back and waves before I catch her arm.

"What the hell are you talking about?"

Her brow furrows. "I mean, I get it that you need to go..."

I scowl at her. "Aren't you going to come? I'm sure Violet is going to be there." In the past, she didn't want to come to the after-game parties. I figured that since we were together—even if it was secret—it would be different and that she'd want to spend time with me because I want to spend time with her.

Now, though, I wonder if she feels that way. Maybe we're truly the same as we were before, only sometimes we spend time in the sack together. As I consider that possibility, my stomach sours. All the excitement from the game is replaced with something sick.

More, I realize that all the confusion and questions are my own fault. I agreed to this stupid with-benefits bullshit.

"Do you want me to come?" Her voice is small, unsure, and I grit my teeth.

"Of course." Is she crazy? Where has she been the last week? "Do you want to come?"

She nods repeatedly. "Yes. Absolutely. If you want me to go."

"Why the hell wouldn't I want you to go?"

"I mean, I don't know." She leans closer. "We're together, but we're not really together. I'd definitely go if I was your real girlfriend. I'd assume you'd want me to go, but I'm not really your girlfriend, so I don't know if I should or shouldn't go." She shifts her weight between her feet and blushes.

I try to follow what she said, but I'm not sure I did. "What do you want to do?"

"What?"

"I want you to be with me." It's my truth. I always want to be with her. "But I know you don't love these parties. What do you want to do?"

She blinks up at me. "I want to be where you are."

The words cause joy like I've never felt before to explode through me. I'm sure she means for this night, but hearing her say that... it's too close to everything I want.

I swallow hard, forcing all that down. "Then let's go to this party." I throw my arm over her shoulders. I've done the same thing dozens of times in the past, before we became more than friends. But this time, she curls against me in a way that's new.

Shea's right—it's time to tell Colt. Very soon.

Shea

A WEEK LATER, JACKIE folds her hands on the table at a bistro in downtown Southampton. "I'm glad you agreed to have lunch with me today."

I smile back. "It's wonderful to see you again." It's been a nice lunch. I always enjoy conversations with Jackie. We spent most of the lunch talking about my classes and how the market for new construction and home renovation looks right now. It's always illuminating to hear Jackie's perspective on how people will adjust their real estate investment dollars over the coming years.

Linc wanted to see his mother this weekend, and I offered to go home with him. He said she's trying a new treatment for her multiple sclerosis, but it needs to be a quick trip. He had games on both Friday and Saturday night. We packed up early on Sunday morning for the four-hour drive home.

I dropped Linc at his parents' house before I drove on to Southampton to meet with Jackie. He seemed distant, and I get the feeling he's still not sleeping well, but every time I ask him what's wrong, he smiles and avoids the questions.

I don't push him too hard, though, because the rest of the week has been perfect. Well, almost perfect. We still haven't told anyone about us, and though it was my idea to keep it a secret, now that feels like a mistake. It's not that I don't love spending time with Linc—I definitely do. But it's getting difficult to pretend we're platonic around everyone else. Justin wasn't much on spontaneous affection. He didn't cuddle, and he'd flinch sometimes if I caught him off guard with a hug or caress. Linc's so physical all the time, constantly touching me, and it's brought me out of my shell. I don't want to hide any of that. I don't want to hide how I feel about him.

Every time I've suggested we tell our families and our friends, he agrees. But he says the timing isn't right. He wants to wait until further in the hockey season, or he wants to tell our family in person. Or he talks about his mom's treatment. All of it sounds like a load of excuses. More likely, he's not comfortable yet with our change in relationship. With more time, he'll come around to the idea. I hope.

Jackie waves her finger toward the waiter. "Would you like some coffee?"

"That sounds good," I say, smiling. We're supposed to drive back to school this evening. I'll need the caffeine.

When the waiter is headed to the kitchen, she levels me with a piercing gaze. "I'd like to make you an official job offer." She pushes a manila envelope across the table that still has our dessert dishes on it.

I gaze at the envelope in front of me with equal parts unease and excitement.

"Why don't you take a look at it, and we can talk over the details?"

I unlatch the envelope and pull out a stack of papers. The first one is a pretty standard employment contract. But the next stack of papers is different. "This looks like an investment opportunity."

Jackie nods. "Yes. I hope you'll hear me out. I've wanted to expand my business for quite some time and now feels like the right opportunity. I'd like to open two additional satellite offices, one in Brooklyn and one in Manhattan. I've included the market research for those two demographics, and I believe that there is enough potential demand there to warrant those locations. I'd like to start in Brooklyn because I believe it's an easier market to crack. And I would like you to oversee running that branch for a thirty-seventy investment split."

"Thirty percent to me, seventy to you." I read the details off the paper.

"Yes." She taps her fingers on the table, the only indication that she's at all uncertain. "My problem is that I am in need of capital."

Into the pause, I finish for her. "You would like me to provide that for you." That was the part of the opportunity where I stopped reading. For me to sign on for this job—manager of her office branch in Brooklyn—she would need a cash capital investment.

Jackie nods. "Yes. I would. We can discuss the initial investment, but I believe we are looking at around a quarter of a million dollars."

I can only blink at her. "Exactly how do you expect me to come up with those funds? I haven't even graduated from college yet." Except I'm not a fool. I know exactly what she's about to say.

She doesn't disappoint. "If you don't have the money in your own name, I would like you to approach your father on our behalf."

I push the stack of business papers away from me a few inches, laughing. "This is not at all what I was expecting you to say today."

Jackie leans forward, her eyes determined. "I like you, Shea. You're good with the customers, you have an amazing eye, and our work ethic is similar. I believe that we could create a beneficial partnership. But there are a couple things that I don't think you know about the workings of a business like mine, including the initial outpour of money that was needed to start it." She presses back into her chair. "I can see how this might come as a shock to you, but after you look over the paperwork, I think you'll see that this is a beneficial opportunity. You enjoy this work. And I can see how we can grow my business together."

"My father—"

"I'm sure that he's going to want to meet with me and that the details of a transaction like this are much more elaborate. But this is where we begin." She places both her hands on top of my employment contract. She gives all the paperwork a push toward me. "Please. Consider what's on the table here."

I nod and gather the papers together, tucking them back inside the envelope. Jackie's face splits into a grin as the waiter arrives with our coffee.

The rest of the lunch is uneventful, and when we leave, Jackie folds me into a hug, promising to be in touch in the coming weeks. I leave with the envelope of paperwork in my tote, feeling like it's an explosive device I'm carrying around.

I check my phone, and there's another text from Justin. This is the third one this week, asking to talk. I delete it without responding. I don't have anything to say to him.

On my way back to Hampton Bays to pick up Linc, I consider Jackie's offer. It isn't what I expected. She told me she wanted me to work for her, but I anticipated the kind of entry-level job offer my peers at CU are getting. Mediocre salary, benefits, and a retirement plan. This is a reminder that I'm not like they are.

I never would have expected Jackie to be someone who tried to use me as an inroad to my father's money, but I don't know why I'm surprised. She's a smart and savvy businesswoman. It would have been a missed opportunity if she hadn't. The expansions to her business sound thrilling, and I'm excited for her.

Whether it's what I want is another story.

Running a satellite office sounds like a wonderful challenge, even if it's impossible not to wonder if she would have given me the opportunity if I didn't have the potential benefit of my father's wealth to bring to the table. I haven't read through the market research, but I've been to Brooklyn enough to recognize that there are plenty of historic homes that I would love to work on.

I'll need to read through the documents carefully. It's a huge decision, and it's made more complicated by my concerns about Jackie's intentions.

After I do my own research, I'll need to figure out a way to loop my father in.

Linc

MY MOTHER LOOKS LIKE shit. She'd probably say the same for me. I can't seem to sleep these days.

Avery called after Mom's treatment on Wednesday and said that it made Mom really sick, so I decided I needed to see her. I figured that would help loosen the anxiety that had taken up residence in my chest.

Not only is Mom pale, but her skin is drawn and dull. I suspect it's pain that's creasing the skin around her eyes, and I hate it. Avery told me that they shaved her hair short before the treatment last week, but I wasn't prepared for how patchy it would look. She's curled into a chair in the corner of the living room, wrapped in the quilt my nana made years ago.

"Are you sure you're not hungry?" I ask, motioning toward the kitchen. It looks like my dad and Avery stocked the place with all her favorites. My parents don't buy much junk food, but I can see Oreos, Cheetos, and a bag of Twix fun-sized candies from here.

She shakes her head. "Even the thought of food makes me queasy right now."

"Well, Mom, you should have said something this morning before I left school. I could have brought some weed for you." I waggle my eyebrows, teasing her. In bad situations, that's what my family does. We joke. "That'd help your appetite."

She gives a bark of laughter. For a moment, she looks exactly like the mom I left behind to go to college a couple of months ago, and that eases me some. "Don't tell me stuff like that. I like to think that you spend all your time at school studying and playing hockey."

"Oh, I absolutely do." I nod solemnly. "Lots of studying. And hockey."

"Right," she says, her lips still twitching. "I saw that Shea dropped you off. How's she doing?" She tilts her head. "She recovered from her breakup in the spring?"

"She's good, Mom. Really good," I answer too quickly and with too much enthusiasm. I grit my teeth. No way she'll let that go without a comment.

She pins me with a stare that sees through me. "Good." I can almost see the wheels turning in her brain. "You know, I always liked the Carmichaels. So much money in that family, but they never come off as entitled or spoiled. Good people."

I'm not sure where this is going, but I'm instantly guarded. "Then you really don't know Colt very well. He's a cocky asshole."

"Pot and kettle, my love."

She has a point. I smother my grin. "Fair enough."

"But Shea... well, I always got the feeling there was something more there. Between the two of you." She raises her eyebrows.

My mother is very intuitive. It can be a real curse. I try to wave her off. "Mom... She's my best friend's sister. And she just spent four years dating someone else. How can there be anything between us?" I shift in my seat on the couch, staring at my hands.

"Yeah. I know all that."

Shea and I are a secret, but there's a difference between not telling people and actively lying. My mom's not feeling well, and she is my mother. I can't lie directly to her face. I never could, and I don't want to start now. I sigh. "You're right."

"I am?"

"Usually. But yeah. There's something between Shea and me. We're kind of..." I don't know how to explain it. "Fuck buddies" isn't a thing I'd ever say to my mother. But also, it's not how I'd describe what's happening, either, even though I used that term with Shea. Shea's so much more than a casual thing. She's everything. "We're seeing each other," I finish.

"What?" My mom's shock borders on outrage.

"You were the one who called me out," I point out to her.

"Yes, but I didn't think I was right for real." She tucks her blanket closer around her. "When did this happen? Why haven't you said anything?"

"We're keeping it quiet for now," I admit, rubbing the back of my neck.

"Why would you do something like that?" She frowns. "We all love Shea. She's wonderful. And beautiful."

"Well, we're just... trying to find a good time to tell Colt," I hedge.

She picks up her cell phone and holds it out to me. "Right now is always a good time."

I run a hand over my hair. "You know it's not as easy as that."

"I didn't say it would be easy. I said that you need to tell him."

She's not telling me anything I don't know. I shrug and hold my hands up. "I don't know. I just... things are so crazy right now. I'm just now back on the ice and..." I glance at her, all huddled in the chair, and all the things at home that weigh me down come rushing to the forefront. But I don't say that, because in the Reynolds family, we ignore things that are obvious. "And things are crazy at school and whatever." I exhale. "I have a lot going on."

"What does that have to do with Shea?"

Telling Colt is going to create a lot of drama, and I'm not sure I can handle anything else right now. I don't want to drag my baggage around in Shea's life. But I can't really say any of that, either. I'm not sure how. So, I only shrug.

"There are things that should stay hidden, baby. But not love. Never that."

I don't want to argue with her. She's doesn't feel well. She doesn't need to hear all my anxieties and worries. "I'm going to heat you up some chicken broth. You need to eat something."

She rolls her eyes and grumbles, but I get up anyway and head into the kitchen. It gives me an excuse to get away from this discussion and my mother's discerning gaze.

As I put the bowl of soup into the microwave, I glance back into the living room and find that she's dozed off.

Both Dad and Avery are working today, and my two younger sisters are with my grandparents until this evening. They'll be back tonight so they can go to school in the morning. I'm glad I'm here and that Mom doesn't have to spend the day alone. She seems too fragile right now.

I talked with my father right after her first treatment earlier this week. He said that the doctors are hopeful that these drugs will help her go into remission and stay there. He sounded hopeful, too, and excited, even though he admitted that my mother's body didn't deal well with the chemotherapy.

But when I talked to Avery again on Friday before my game, she wasn't as optimistic. She said that even though Mom was a stellar candidate for this kind of therapy, the costs were astronomical. Both Avery and Dad were working overtime to help save up money, but they still weren't sure how they'd be able to handle the expenses. She graduates from high school this year, and though I'm pushing her to apply to colleges, I get the feeling she's only agreeing to investigate it because she doesn't want to argue with me.

My heart starts racing, and I recognize the beginning of a panic attack. I try to breathe, but it's hard to catch my breath, hard to think around the sense of impending doom.

I stand there for a long time, struggling to breathe, leaving my mother's soup in the microwave to stay warm while she naps and wondering exactly how this is all going to be okay in the end.

Shea

I PARK IN FRONT of Linc's parents' house in Hampton Bays and catch Avery on her way inside. I don't know Linc's oldest sister well, but she's always struck me as level-headed and too mature for her age. She stops on the porch and smiles, but it's obvious she's tired. I hurry to catch up, reaching to help her with her stuff. "What's all this?" I ask.

"Clothes, towel, lunch bag, and purse." She hoists her gym bag onto my shoulder. "I lifeguarded a swim meet at the pool today then taught swimming lessons this afternoon."

That's right. Linc said that Avery swam on a club team and her school team. "How was it?"

"As good as you can expect from five-year-old kids who are afraid of the water. We worked on putting their faces in and floating on their backs."

I grin. "Sounds exciting."

"They're actually adorable," Avery offers with a smile. "Just nervous." She pushes through the door, her smile fades, and she tenses. Her eyes scan the living room, and she looks back, her finger on her lips to ask me not to speak.

Mrs. Reynolds must be sleeping. I stall in the doorway, not sure if I should come inside. Avery waves me in, though, and we creep down the hall, past the living room, and into the kitchen at the back of the house.

I glance into the living room, and the sight of Linc's mother is shocking. Her head is shaved, and she's pale. I contemplate what kind of treatment would make her look like this.

I love the Reynolds' house. It's a 1920s Craftsman with a huge front porch. But it's not only the architecture that I love. It always smells good, because the Reynolds family eats together all the time. Everything in the place is touchable too. There's leather furniture in the living room with lots of pillows and throw blankets. The fireplace is original to the house, stone from ceiling to floor, and it's well used.

The kitchen isn't trendy, but it's homey. There's a peninsula in the center. I remember when Mr. Reynolds refinished their cabinets and added a soapstone counter even before that was stylish. He said that if soapstone was good enough for research laboratories, it was safe enough for his family of six.

But Linc isn't inside. Avery drops her stuff on the counter and points at the back door. I go through to a porch that's almost as big as the one out front. I find him sitting at the table there, a glass of iced tea in front of him. "Hey."

"Hey," he says, reaching for his drink. "I made tea if you want some."

"I'm good for now." I settle in the seat next to his. "How's your mom?"

He shakes his head. I can't read his mood right now, and it's unsettling.

"I saw she's sleeping," I offer. "Exactly what kind of treatment —"

"It's chemotherapy, Tiny." He turns the glass on the table a half turn then another. "She's having chemotherapy."

I try to rationalize that. Mrs. Reynolds has multiple sclerosis, not cancer. Why would they be treating her with chemotherapy?

"My mom's flare-ups have gotten increasingly worse over the past few years, debilitating even. The doctors believe that this treatment plan will help stop their frequency, even send her into remission."

"Jesus, Linc..." I stare at him. "Why didn't you say something?" I've asked him loads of times over the past months and years how his mother was. He's been vague, offering short answers, barely giving me any information. When he said that he wanted to come and see her this weekend, I had no idea that things were so bad.

"You don't need to hear all the gory details of what's going on with me." He leans forward, retrieves his glass, and takes another sip of his drink.

"You should know me better than that. I care about you. I want to hear all the details of what's going on with you." I can't believe he kept something like this from me. "Have you said anything to Colt?"

He shrugs. "You know how brutal his schedule is."

That's a no, then. I frown. "You didn't tell either of us about your panic attacks, either, not until I practically stumbled on them." My tone sounds accusing, and I pause to take a deep breath. "Why didn't you say something?"

"You guys don't need to know all this shitty stuff. Hell, I barely want to know it. I definitely don't want to share it."

I hate his self-deprecating tone. I grind my teeth, trying to stave off my frustration. "We're your friends. Of course, we want to hear about it all. Or"—I pause, narrowing my eyes at him—

"if you told us, you'd need to accept our help, and God forbid you ever ask anyone for help."

He scowls at me. "What does that mean?"

"You're always there for us, but then you hide stuff like this. Why?" He drops his gaze to his lap and shakes his head. I'm not going to get an answer out of him. He might not even have an answer.

It seems like I've known him my entire life, but there have been quite a few times in the last month when I've looked at him and felt like I was seeing a stranger. I'm always an open book, and it's hard for me to think that he's hiding things from me, especially if he doesn't even realize he does it.

We sit in silence for long minutes, and I try to think about what I can say to get through to him. If it was only me, I might take it more personally, but it's Colt too. I doubt he's told any of his other hockey friends either. Not Declan or Cord Spellman. How can you convince someone to let people in?

"Does your family need anything?" I eventually ask. He has relatives around—I've been to barbecues with his grandparents and aunts and uncles—and I'm glad that they're not far removed from people who can help them.

"Yeah, they need me to sign a contract with the Gladiators. Like, yesterday."

"What do you mean?"

He finally looks over at me. "My father is self-employed. My mom lost her medical benefits when she had to stop working. Our health insurance isn't great." He pauses, tugging at the edge of his shorts. "Her chemotherapy is expensive. When I sign my contract, I'll be able to help them out."

I narrow my eyes. "How bad is it?"

He sighs. "Something like twenty-five grand."

Money has never been a thing I think of much. My mother came from old money in Georgia, and my father was already well-off when they married. Their situation only improved from there. I don't know what it's like to struggle financially, and I hate that Linc does.

"My family... we can help yours." His face storms over, but I keep talking. I need to do something. This is Linc. "What if there's someone my parents know? Someone who can help. And money..."

He stands up, digging his hands into his hair. "No. No money. Nothing."

"Linc."

"This is one of the reasons I haven't said anything to you guys. Because I want to be your friend, not the Carmichaels' charity case." He drops a hand to his waist. "Your father put in a good word for me when I was looking at colleges. Did you know that? No one with my high school grades could have gotten into CU. But it's his alma mater. I know he helped, I bet even with the financial aid I received."

"You got a sports scholarship." I don't know if what he suggests about my father is true. I never asked about that. But I do know that Linc's one of the team's top athletes. His money to play is well-earned.

"For room and board, Shea. My tuition is paid for by a private scholarship." He paces the porch. "And I lost my room-and-board money this year, thanks to the concussions. I needed to come up with that money. Even with roommates, our rent's not cheap."

"Jesus, Linc..."

"Exactly, Shea. But my family and I, we're handling it. We'll handle this too." He opens the back door and goes inside, leaving me on the porch by myself.

I stare out into his backyard, completely unsettled.

The picture he paints is bleak, and I had no idea what he was going through. I try not to let that bother me, but it does. He worked a lot this summer, but I thought he was only helping his father. I had no idea things were this bad for them.

I'm sure there's something I can do. If he doesn't want money, fine. There must be something else. I'll figure out some way to help.

I want to tell Colt. He'd back me up. This is Linc we're talking about. But I can't exactly tell him all of this without giving away exactly how close Linc and I have become. I grit my teeth. Right now, holding all this in is harder than it should have to be.

I open the door and go into the kitchen to find that Linc's father is home. "Hey, Shea. How are you?"

"Good, Mr. Reynolds," I respond automatically. If he notices I'm stiff, he doesn't say anything. He's got other things on his mind, I'm sure.

"We're going to order pizza. Can you guys stay for dinner?" he asks Linc.

Linc glances at me quickly and then away. "I don't know, Dad..."

"We have an hour, I think." I smile at his father. "I'd like to say hello to your wife, too, if she wakes."

"Sounds good." His dad looks tired, but his grin is genuine.

We all make small talk quietly, so we don't wake Linc's mother until it's time to get the pizza. I offer to do the pickup, and Linc follows me out to the car. As we slide into my Audi, he covers my hand with his, stopping me from turning on the car. "I'm sorry, Shea. I didn't mean to snap at you earlier."

I smile and sigh. One thing about Linc Reynolds—he's extremely predictable. Always a quick apology. I've never seen him hold a grudge, and he's always the first to say he's sorry. It's one of many things I adore about him. "It's okay. I only wish you'd told me some of this. You don't have to do this all alone. Even if you just let me be someone to talk to. I just... I want to help. And Colt would too. I wish you'd said something."

"I know. I get it. But I can take care of this on my own."

I don't understand why he needs to. Linc's always been private, but we've slept together and have spent so much time together. I don't understand why he refused even to share this with me.

We drive to the pizza place, both lost in thought. When we return to his parents' house, though, his mother is awake. What follows is the kind of dinner I expect at the Reynolds—loud and full of laughter and love. His mother might look frail, but she's as feisty as ever. Whatever tension there is between Linc and me dissipates as we tease and joke around at dinner.

When we finally get back to my place later that night, our lovemaking feels different. It's still amazing between us. I could never have imagined I was missing the kind of chemistry that I've found with him. But tonight, there's a desperate edge to it. I can't tell whether the new anxiety is coming from me or from him. It could be both of us.

In the darkness afterward, I curl into his side and silently hope that tomorrow, everything will look better.

Shea

"THIS LOOKS EXACTLY AS you described." Violet hands over the manila envelope that Jackie gave me at lunch the other day. "She wants you to invest a sum to be determined in exchange for thirty percent of her company and for you to take a leadership role in the Brooklyn branch of her business."

I nod. That was how I read the documents as well. "She wants my father to invest that money and buy me the partial ownership and leadership role in her business."

Violet bites her lower lip, not saying anything. Like me, her mother comes from old money. Except, while Violet had access to a trust fund at eighteen, my parents still act as executors of any money in my name for another six years. Though they're not very strict with my daily spending, I can't imagine that my dad wouldn't notice a quarter of a million dollars gone missing.

"What am I going to do?" I ask my friend.

She shrugs. "What do you want to do?"

"I don't want to do corporate design. I know that for sure." We're sitting at a deli in downtown Chesterboro. I bought Violet lunch in exchange for her using her business degree to check over my paperwork. We could have had this conversation in the cafeteria, but I needed a break from Linc and the hockey boys.

As far as I can tell, Linc's barely sleeping, and when he does, he tosses and turns. He's not eating much, either, which is strange. I'm really starting to worry about him. Still, he doesn't say much about it. It's like he's determined to hold it all together, even while he's strung out.

I wish he would talk with me more about it. But you can't force someone to talk if they don't want to.

My phone buzzes on the table next to me. I glance at it then delete the latest text from Justin, growling at my phone.

"Was that Justin?" Violet asks. She must have seen his name pop up.

"Yeah. He's been bugging me to talk since the gala in New York. I should block him."

"What does he want? Have you told him that you're with Linc now?"

"I haven't told anyone that I'm with Linc."

She casts me an offended look.

"Except you." Violet helped me talk through my feelings for him before the gala, so she was obviously interested to find out how things went when I told her he was there. She's my closest friend. I trust her not to say anything. "It's not that I don't want to tell everyone, because I do. I told Linc that we should tell our families at Thanksgiving next Thursday. He still hasn't agreed, but he hasn't said no yet either."

"Thanksgiving, huh?" She shrugs. "Well, that'll keep discussion away from politics, I guess."

I laugh, but it dies a moment later. "I wish things were easier with him right now. I know he's got a lot going on, but keeping our relationship a secret doesn't feel right anymore." I sigh. "I almost feel like he doesn't want to tell anyone."

"At all?" Violet scowls. "No way. He's crazy about you. The way he looks at you? Guys don't just do that. I can see it as clear as day."

"It's not that I don't think he cares about me. It's just... he can be closed off. I feel like things are going great with us, but we're stuck in some weird limbo."

"And you want more," she finishes softly.

My eyes sting, and I swallow my tears, nodding. I'm a fool. This summer, I was sure I didn't want a boyfriend. But that was before Linc. Now, I'd do anything to have him call me his girlfriend.

"Hang in there, girl," she says, pushing the rest of her cheesecake across the table to me. I take a big bite. "You're happy being with him, aren't you?"

"I am." More than I ever would have imagined.

"Then you may need to wait for him on this one."

"Aren't you the one who's always telling me I should ask for what I want?" I point at her with my fork.

"You did that already. Now, you need to wait for him to catch up to you." She shrugs. "In relationships, it's not all about you or all about them. It's got to be both. And when it is?" She sighs. "Well, then it can be magic."

I only stare at her, sipping my coffee again. I'm not exactly sure what she means, but she's right about one thing: I can't force Linc to be ready for a true, open relationship with me.

But I can't shake the feeling that I might be asking for too much from him. And if I am, I'm not sure what that means for us.

Linc

WE HAVE TWO GAMES the weekend before Thanksgiving. I'm glad about the upcoming holiday with my family. I'm wound too tightly. I need to get my thoughts together, and I'm looking forward to seeing my mother again. The word from home is that she's been doing better, but I'll feel more comfortable after I see for myself.

Friday night, we're on the road against State, and it's always nice to beat them, especially in their building. I'm creating some great chemistry with Griffin, and we aren't on the ice for either of State's goals. We win 4-2.

Saturday, no one talks about the fact that we're undefeated, but it hangs over us in our locker room. Winning streaks are strange creatures. When they visit you, you don't want to make a big deal about them, but you don't want to do anything to offend them, either, so everyone tries to play it cool and not rock the boat. Hockey players are superstitious people. Things are going right, so that means some guys aren't washing their socks or jerseys. Hell, some of the guys don't smell like they've showered, but no one is complaining. I don't even hear any grumbles when Mike Dischenski plays "Sweet Caroline" before the game—again. We're all invested. "Keep it loose and even" is the mantra in the locker room tonight.

The first period is more of what we've been doing. We get up by a goal right before the first intermission. At the beginning of the second period, though, it's clear that our opponents aren't happy about the score. They're playing with more fire than before, like they went into their locker room at the break and found some inspiration. They score two goals quickly to take the lead, including one on a breakaway that I should have prevented.

Squelching frustration at my sloppy play, I line up for the face-off. Ash wins it back to me, and I deke around the forward who confronts me for the puck. Skating wide, I reach to sling the puck off the boards and into our zone as their defender checks me.

I'm off balance and overreaching, and the hit is awkward. Nothing dirty, but I'm balanced on one skate when the defenseman hits me, and my leg kicks out behind me.

I land on the ice in a heap and slide into the boards. I always tell my family that the loud hits on the boards aren't the ones that hurt. The boards flex so they absorb some of the shock. But the bottom of the rink's border is concrete. When you hit that, it doesn't make a sound, and it hurts like a bitch.

The bounce I take sucks the air out of my lungs, even as I curl around the burst of pain in my groin. I gasp, trying to drag some oxygen into my body and think straight. I need to get off the ice. My team needs a fifth skater. Even as I think it, a groan goes up through the stadium. I glance up to see the goal light flashing over my goalie's shoulder. Damn it, it's 3-1.

I struggle to get to my knees, still sucking wind, and the trainer, Tom, appears at my side. "How we doing here,

Reynolds?" Tom and I are tight, thanks to last year's concussions.

"Not sure I'll ever father children, Tom," I gasp out.

Tom's brows crease. "That's no good. You think you can stand?"

I nod and shift to my feet, even as pain shoots through my groin again. I know better than to give too much away here, though. The entire stadium of people watches me. I lean heavily on Tom's shoulder and do my best not to let my limp look too pronounced as we shuffle off the ice. Vaguely, I can hear my teammates banging their sticks against the boards. As I head toward the locker room, my eyes search our seats, connecting with Shea. The concern on her face almost buckles my knees.

Tom and I stumble together down the ramp and into the locker room. Two assistant trainers meet us at the door, and they help me into the training room and up onto an exam table. There's more jostling around as they efficiently set to work on my skates and shin guards then take off my hockey pants. When my gear is off, Tom starts checking me over. He shines a light into my eyes. "Good news. Doesn't look like a concussion."

I'm still breathing heavily, trying to get air into my chest. "That's something." I wince. "But I think my dick's on fire."

One of the assistant trainers chuckles as Tom grins at me. "I'm getting there." I wait patiently as he checks my shoulders, my ribs, and my arms. But when he presses into my left groin, I flinch. "Shit."

"Definitely some kind of groin pull or strain. Let's hope it's not a tear of any kind," Tom says, still glancing me over with clinical precision.

I nod, gritting my teeth. As he continues, nothing else appears out of place, but the ramifications of a groin injury settle over me. I'm going to be off the ice, and I'm not sure for how long. This couldn't have come at a worse time. We're in the middle of a winning streak, and I'm trying to pressure my agent to go to bat for me with the Gladiators. The last thing I need is to be humping the bench again.

"Let's get you down the hall, take some pictures, and see what we're dealing with here." Tom pats my shoulder, finished with his exam. He offers me a reassuring grin. "There's no need to panic yet. Let's take it one step at a time."

What follows is a flurry of X-rays and an MRI. They confirm Tom's suspicions. It's only a strain, thank God. It still means I might be out until after the New Year, but it's not something that will cause permanent damage.

I hope.

By the time I get back to my phone, Shea's blown it up with a dozen texts. I call her. "Hey."

"Linc. Are you okay?"

Her worry hits me in the gut, and I close my eyes, upset I didn't think to check my phone sooner. "I'm okay, Tiny. A strained groin muscle. First degree. They didn't see any tears."

"Only a strain?" She's been around hockey most of her life. She saw my overreach and knows how bad it could have been. Injuries are part of the game, though. Most players have them at some point in their careers.

"That's what they think."

She exhales shakily. "Thank God."

"Yeah."

"You're still with the trainers?" she asks.

"Yeah. I'm going to sit in an ice bath for a while. Are you still here?" The game has been over for at least half an hour. I'm an asshole. I was so caught up in my own head, I didn't think about how upset she might be.

"I am. Violet stayed with me. Declan came out a bit ago and told us it didn't seem too serious, but I wanted to hear it from you."

"I'm okay. Really. Why don't you head home? I'll see you tomorrow."

"Are you sure?"

"I'm sure." Guilt rides me. I hate how anxious she sounds. This isn't all from this injury. She's worrying about me, and I hate it. I'm restless and distracted, and she notices. Of course she does—we're together all the time.

"I'll stop by tomorrow."

I pause before saying, "Sure." But I'm uneasy. I hate the idea of her having to take care of me. This injury is just one more thing to worry about. Sighing, I hang up then toss my phone into my bag before heading back to the ice bath.

I'm trying so hard to pull the threads of my life together, but the harder I try, the more it seems to be falling apart around me.

Linc

I DON'T MAKE IT home for Thanksgiving until late on Wednesday night. I wanted to eke out another day with my mom and get here yesterday, but I had a study session after lunch on Wednesday. It's almost finals, and I need the help. I've been struggling to concentrate in my classes lately. But now that means this trip will be a flyby because I need to be back at school on Friday for a game. Though I'm not playing, thanks to the groin pull, I'd never miss a game.

Everyone's asleep by the time I get in, so I don't see anyone until breakfast on Thanksgiving morning. The kitchen already smells like coffee when I get downstairs, and my mother looks light years better than she did the last time I saw her. It's a huge relief. "Morning, love," she says. "I bought danish, and I have bacon. Coffee's about done."

I settle gingerly on a stool at the island. My groin pull already feels much better, but I'm still taking it easy. "Are you sure you should be up and around like this? Why don't you let me make the bacon?" I offer.

"I'm feeling fine, honey. I promise. Besides, you have a groin strain. You shouldn't be up and moving too much." She reaches over to pat my cheek. It's still a shock to see her hair this short, but the color on her cheeks and sharpness in her eyes convince me that she's not lying. "I'll take a break if I need to."

"Definitely."

"But right now, I'm going to make bacon, and then I need you to help me make apple pie to take over to the Carmichaels." I saw the pumpkin pie in the refrigerator last night. It smelled like cinnamon heaven. My mother knows her way around desserts.

"It's nice of them to invite us over."

"Yes. Very kind. Your father offered to fry the turkey here, but I'm glad that's unnecessary now. Lena Carmichael saved me from having to call the fire department later."

This isn't the first time that we've spent a holiday with their family. Mrs. Carmichael tries to get as many of Colt's people together as she can when he's in town. For Thanksgiving the last two years, Colt's game schedule had him out of state. He's at home tomorrow in Philadelphia, so he'll be at dinner with his family.

I'm glad I'll get to spend the day with Shea too. She came over on Sunday to keep me company, but I was sore and grouchy. I hate being hurt, and I'm not a good patient. It makes me feel useless. Since then, we've exchanged texts, but I always feel like she wants me to say more. She asks how I'm doing, what I'm thinking, how I'm feeling. Questions like that require emotional energy, and I'm not sure how to answer them. I don't want to tell her how scared I am that this injury might mess up my year. I don't want to talk about how angry it makes me that my body is screwing up my chances to help my family because if I talk about it, it'll make all the uncertainty more real. I prefer to ignore that and focus on what I can do—dig in to physical therapy, take it easy, and keep my chin up.

I'll need to apologize to her when I see her today. I've been short-tempered and broody all week. I've been apologizing to her a lot recently.

I do agree with her about one thing—tonight, we need to tell Colt about our relationship. I said I'd stay after dinner so we can tell him together.

I try not to worry about that and instead focus on helping my mom with breakfast and pie baking.

My younger sisters join in when they get up, and before long, the kitchen is full of Christmas music and the smell of cinnamon, and I feel more like my old self than I have in a long time. My father turns on the Macy's parade, and the mood is lighter than it's been in months. I tease my sisters, and when the pie goes in the oven, my father and I sit down to watch some football before we all get dressed to go to the Carmichaels'.

I drive separately so I can stay after dinner with Shea and Colt, and my parents follow me to their house. When we pull into the drive to their house, though, it seems that we're not the only ones that Mrs. Carmichael has invited to dinner. There are two other cars already parked, a Benz and a BMW. The BMW looks vaguely familiar.

When I kill the engine on my car, my phone's Do Not Disturb goes off, and I get two texts in quick succession.

Colt: *My mom invited the fucking Petersons for dinner too.*

Colt: *Apparently the douchebag broke up with his fiancée.*

Shea

I'M GOING TO KILL my mother. I cannot believe she didn't tell me the Petersons were coming. Not that this situation is all her fault. It's not. She doesn't know I'm with Linc, because we haven't said anything. So, she doesn't know how awkward this might be. That's on Linc and me.

Melanie Peterson is one of her best friends. When her son's engagement breaks off, obviously my mother would step in and offer to host them for the next major holiday.

I grit my teeth as the Petersons step inside and we take their coats. Justin hangs back from his parents, and I know he wants to talk to me. He's been texting me for weeks. He stands awkwardly next to me, chewing on his lip.

I need to say something, I guess. I settle on, "Happy Thanksgiving, Justin." I smile, but it feels wooden. Colt appears at my side.

"Peterson," he says.

"Thanks for having us." He looks as uncomfortable as I feel, and I wonder if he's the victim of our parents as much as I am.

"How have you been?" I ask into the silence that follows, because it's polite, and there's nothing else to say.

"I've been okay," he offers, but he winces.

"I'm sorry to hear about Isabella." I figure it's probably easier to get the awkwardness out of the way.

Colt snorts, his lips twisting into a smirk. I scowl up at him because that's not nice. For his part, Justin looks like he swallowed a lemon.

"Kids, why don't we all move into the living room for a drink?" My mom steps in, smooth as ever. "The Reynolds will be here in a few minutes, I'd imagine."

"I'll wait for them," I offer quickly, sending my mother a pleading look.

"Of course," she says with a smile. "Come." She motions to the Petersons. "I made a cranberry punch." They follow her, but Colt stays with me. I sigh with relief.

"Christ, I can't believe she invited them." I shake my head.

"You can't?"

"Fine, I can. But God, this is awful."

He doesn't even know half of it yet. Still, he nods sympathetically. Then he wrinkles his nose, glancing out the window. "Hey, did you know that Linc's mom is going through some treatments or something? He said she needed to shave her head. Do you know anything about that?" He shakes his head. "I swear, that guy never tells me anything that's bothering him."

I can only shrug. It isn't my news to share.

Lights in the drive signal the Reynolds are here, right on time. I press my palm to my forehead and smooth my cashmere sweater as I open the door, stepping onto the porch to wait for them. Colt follows me. We greet them, passing hugs around as Colt ushers them inside, taking their coats. I snag Linc's arm and save my hug for him for last.

I can't help worrying about his appearance. He's gorgeous, as always, in tan pants and a navy sweater. But he looks thinner, somehow, and there are dark circles under his eyes. I step into his arms. "How are you?" I ask.

"I hear Peterson is here," he murmurs in my ear.

"My mother didn't tell me she was inviting him," I mutter back.

"I figured. You okay?" He asks, squeezing my hand. Of course, he's worrying about me.

I grit my teeth, trying to attempt a grin. Everything is easier with him here. By the end of the night, I'll tell my family about us. We won't need to pretend anymore. "I'm great."

He chuckles, but it doesn't reach his eyes.

"What's up, guys?" Colt interrupts us from the door. I step away from Linc quickly, as if I got caught doing something wrong. That irritates me, though, and I need to take a deep breath before I respond.

"We're on our way in. How's it going in there?"

Colt glances between the two of us, a question on his face. "Could use some reinforcements." He holds his hand out to Linc. "Good to see you. How's your mom?"

"She's doing well. Better, I think." Colt and I wait, giving him room to say more. He doesn't, so Colt clears his throat.

"Let's get in there, then."

Cocktails go fine. My mother's punch is delicious. Justin stays with our parents, and Colt and I end up chatting with the Reynolds. It isn't until my mother calls us in to dinner that things get awkward.

The table is beautiful. My mom has outdone herself. I can appreciate the aesthetic, all gold, copper, and rust. She broke out the china she got for her wedding, and it's beautiful. Cornucopias and corn husks, all sorts of holiday decor.

That's not the problem.

She's seated me next to Justin and his family. I grit my teeth even as I keep a smile on my face. I try to figure out if there's some way I can rearrange the place settings and get out of what is undoubtedly going to be an awkward meal. Linc is placed at the other end of the table with his family. He isn't looking at us, but I can see the tension in his shoulders as he sits.

There's nothing I can do except take my seat.

After we're all sitting, my mother chats with the Petersons. My father strikes up a conversation with the Reynolds parents, and Colt chats with Linc and his sisters.

That leaves me with Justin.

I flatten my napkin on my lap and reach for my salad fork.

"I've been trying to get ahold of you," he says.

"I know. I've gotten your texts." There's nothing else to say about that. I'm aware that he wants to talk. I don't reciprocate the feeling. I sip my wine. Mom poured a Chardonnay for the first course. It pairs with the salad perfectly. I take another bite, hoping that discourages Justin from saying more.

He pinches his lips together, obviously trying to figure out what to do. He starts again. "Did you have fun at the gala?"

"I did." I reach for some bread. "Did you?"

"Things weren't going well with Isabella, so it could have been better."

I'm not sure why this is something I need to know, but I make an appropriate noise. "That's a shame."

I'm not giving him much to go on, but it's not my job to make him comfortable. He frowns, and my mother must have seen his expression because she asks, "Justin, how is law school going?"

He starts talking, and I continue with my salad, happy to not have to engage for a moment. Down the table, I can feel Linc's eyes on me. His expression is dark. Add that to how tired he looks, and my heart clenches.

Please, let us get through this meal in one piece. Then we can talk to Colt, and things will be better.

Dinner is wonderful—not because my mother can cook. She cannot. She had it catered, and whoever roasted the turkey knew exactly what they were doing. For the rest of the meal, my mother makes sure that Justin and I aren't left to speak alone. She masterfully brings up topics that the Petersons will all participate in. She's really a genius in social situations.

Finally, when we've all eaten our fill, my mother turns to me and asks, "Shea. Would you mind starting the coffee?" She must see that I've had enough of Justin and might need a few minutes alone.

"Of course, Mama." I stand without question, happy to get away.

"I'll help her, Mrs. Carmichael," Justin offers, pushing his chair back.

"Oh, that's all right, Justin. Why don't you go and pour some bourbon for the gentlemen?" Mom suggests.

But Justin doesn't take the hint. "I wouldn't want Shea to have to do this all on her own." He stands, joining me at the door to the kitchen. I clench my jaw and meet my mother's eyes. The look she gives me is part helplessness and part apology.

"Thank you," I mumble, even as my eyes find Linc again. His hands are fists on the table. I can't do anything, though, so I push into the kitchen. Justin follows me, and the door swings closed behind us.

I head to the coffee pot across the room, determined to put as much space between us as possible.

"Shea." He joins me, standing right next to me.

I close my eyes, wishing for deliverance from this conversation.

"Please hear me out."

I sigh, reaching for a new filter. "Why? I don't really care what you have to say." I point at him. "Obviously. Because that's why I didn't text you back."

"I was wrong. I screwed up, baby." He moves closer, rubbing his fingers on my arm. I step away, far enough that he's not touching me. "I'm so sorry."

I cross my arms over my chest. "For what?"

"What?"

"What are you sorry for, Justin? For cheating on me all those times? Because I know it wasn't once or twice. I hear that you spent time with almost all the Tri-Delt sisters. Are you sorry for that?" I touch my lips with my index finger. "Or are you sorry for proposing to a girl after only knowing her for two months?" I tap my temple. "I bet that's not it. You should be sorry for treating me badly for years. But I bet that hasn't crossed your mind."

I want to be able to hold it together, but really, this guy has a lot of nerve. Fine, he's here for the holiday. His parents were invited. But following me in here takes more balls than I expected out of him.

His mouth opens and closes for a moment. I grin, morbidly satisfied that I might have struck him speechless. He recovers quickly, though. "All of that, baby. I'm so sorry."

I blow out a breath. "Please." I put a filter in the machine and go to the refrigerator, where we keep the coffee.

"Give me another chance. I promise that things will be different. I'll be better."

"No, you won't." I meet his eyes. "We both know that the problem is that you're alone, and you can't stand it. My mother said that you and Isabelle broke up. But my guess is that she broke up with you." He doesn't dispute me, and I shake my head, chuckling. "You're a mess."

He steps closer, reaching for me. "I am a mess... because I miss you," he insists. "I want us to try again." He tries to pull me into his arms, but I swat at him, pushing him away.

"Let me go, Justin." I shove him. Did he drink too much? Is that why he's not listening to me right now? More likely, he's not used to girls saying no to him.

"Shea, I've changed." He drops his head into my shoulder and rubs his fingers along my back. I continue pushing him away. But when he moves to kiss me, I panic and knee him in the groin.

He doubles over and falls to the ground, gasping. I pat him on the back. "I'm sorry," I say. "I asked you to..."

I don't get a chance to say anything else because Linc swings me around and pulls me into his arms, every muscle in his body vibrating. "What happened? Are you okay?"

I don't know what he said to excuse himself from the table, but I'm so glad he's here. He smooths my hair back and searches my face, as if he needs to determine for himself that I'm fine.

"Linc," I offer. "I'm good. Really," I add when he doesn't look convinced.

He glances around the kitchen, taking in Justin, who is hunched over. The grim satisfaction on his face shouldn't make me happy, but it does. "Come on." He pushes through the back door, and we step out onto the patio. The only light out here is coming from the kitchen inside.

He runs his fingers over my face, and I curl against him. I smile up at him and step closer, cupping his face with my hands, happy to be in his arms. He breathes in through his nose and out his mouth, like he's trying to control himself. "You're sure you're fine?"

"Way better now." I pull his face closer to mine and kiss him, sighing into his mouth. It's been such a strange week. I've needed him. We kiss softly.

"What's going on here?" Colt stands in the doorway to the kitchen. He pushes out to join us and lets the door swing closed behind him. "Why are you kissing my sister?"

"Colt..." I begin. The tension ratchets up, and I step between my brother and Linc. I don't like the way they're looking at each other. Colt's shoulders are tight, and his hands are fisted. "Calm down."

Linc steps around me, putting himself between my brother and me. A muscle in his jaw flexes again and again. He lifts his hands. "Colt. Let me explain."

Except he doesn't have a chance. Colt hauls off and punches him right in the jaw.

Linc

I COULD SEE THE hit coming, but I wasn't going to do anything about it. The hit throws my head back, and I brace my hands on my knees. "Fuck, Colt. That hurt," I say, wiping a trickle of blood off my lip.

"You were kissing my sister," Colt growls as he kicks me in the ribs. Shea cries out and rushes to my side as I drop to my hands and knees.

"Stand up," Colt snarls behind me. His legs are apart, and his fists are clenched as he looks down at us.

"So you can punch me again?" I gasp.

"Yes," Cowl grits out. "You deserve it."

"Fair enough." I shift, attempting to right myself.

"Colt. Stop it," Shea snaps at him. "He's already had concussions." She tries to help me up, but she wouldn't be able to move me on her own. I do most of the work, even as my face is aching. Shit, that really did hurt.

"He should have thought about his concussions sooner. Like before he started kissing you," Colt shoots over her shoulder at me.

Shea growls at him. "You don't really want to hurt him, you jackass. He's your best friend." She stands close to me, like she'll physically shield me from her own brother.

"I told you he was going to hit me," I tell her. I'm trying to make a joke, but nothing could be less funny. "I win that bet." I swipe again at my mouth. My lip's busted and already starting to swell.

"Goddamn it." Colt paces, his hands on his hips. "You were supposed to keep an eye on her at school. An eye, Linc. Not your whole body." He blows out a disgusted breath, standing right in front of me. "She's my fucking sister."

"I know." I shake my head. "I'm sorry, Colt. I shouldn't have."

Next to me, Shea flinches, her face jerking up to mine. I glance down at her, shaking my head.

"You told me that you'd watch out for her, keep her safe from guys who would take advantage of her. But *you* took advantage of her." He grips the front of my shirt, growling right in my face.

I hold his eyes. "You're right. I did."

"No, you did not. I'm standing right here." Shea stomps her foot, gripping Colt's arm. "I have some say in what I do. And no one took advantage of me."

Colt and I continue to stare at each other. She growls up at us. "Christ. It's like I've traveled back in time to the nineteenth century."

"We didn't mean for it to happen," I offer because I don't have much to defend myself.

Colt shakes me, his hands still fisted in his shirt. "Why the fuck are you messing with her?"

"I love her," I tell him. "I've loved her forever." Beside me, Shea gasps, covering her mouth. I meet her troubled gaze. "I do."

Her eyes fill with tears, and she shakes her head at me. I'm fucking this all up. I can see it on her face. She's been asking to come clean to Colt for weeks, but this isn't how it was supposed to go.

Colt shoves me away from him. "You've lied to me for years. Why should I believe a thing you say?" He waves at Shea. "And you. Why didn't you tell me? I'm your brother."

She wraps her arms around herself, shaking her head at him even as a tear drips out of her eye. "This isn't your business, Colt. You're my brother, and I love you, but you don't get to tell me what I can and can't do with my life."

"Right. Of course. I'm only trying to look out for you." He steps away from both of us.

"Not like this." She ducks her head, shaking it sadly. "This isn't you looking out for me. You're upset that we kept this from you. The way you're acting is about you, not me."

"Maybe, Shea. But at least I didn't lie." He points at us from the patio door. "To either of you." He pushes through the patio door, leaving Shea and me outside alone.

Shit. This is a disaster. I watch him go inside, step over where Justin is still hunched over, and head back into the dining room.

"Shea..." I run a hand over my hair.

She lifts her hand to stop me. "Did you mean it? That you love me? Did you mean that?"

I blow out a shaky breath.

"Did you mean it, Linc?" she presses. "Because you didn't say it to me. You said it to my brother." She looks up at the sky and around the darkened patio, anywhere but at me. "This... this isn't how I expected you to tell me that, if I ever truly expected you to say it at all. It's definitely not how I wanted it. That was a confession to my brother, something you're sorry for, something that you feel guilty about."

I reach for her, but she steps away from me. I hold my hands out to her. "Shea, please. I do." As she shakes her head, my stomach is sick and sour, and everything in my chest feels like it's shattering to pieces. "You have to know that. I love you so much."

"Why would you tell Colt before you tell me?" Her face is flushed, and her voice is so broken it hurts to listen to it. "If you've felt like this for so long, why didn't you say something to me?" She points at herself, jabbing her chest with her finger.

I can only swallow. I don't know what to say.

"Why?" she cries.

"Because I'm a fucking mess!" I fire back at her. "I'm a fucking mess, and you deserve someone who has their shit together." I motion to the kitchen where Justin's finally standing. "That dickhead is in law school. Me? I'm barely sleeping, and my stomach is so tied up these days, I can barely eat. I've got a groin pull now, after a year of concussions. I have no idea if I'll ever be able to pull my hockey career out of the toilet. My mom is sick, and my family is in serious debt. I'm trying to get to a place where I'm not causing you to worry about me all the time. How the hell can I be a good boyfriend to you right now when I'm like this?"

It's everything that's been weighing me down these past months, everything I've been trying to hold together, and all the things I wish I never had to burden her with. "I didn't want to tell Colt because I knew he wouldn't take it well. He's pissed at me and upset with you. So now, not only am I a hot mess on my own, but I've caused drama with your family."

"This could have been much easier," she whispers. "I wanted to be there for you. I wanted to be your girlfriend. I love you, too, Linc, but this... this isn't what I want for me, and it's not what I want for you." She steps forward and places her hand on my cheek. I cover her fingers with mine.

The look on her face is sorrow and pain. Worse, it's goodbye.

"No, Shea, please, listen... we can work on this. I'm trying to fix things. I only need a little more time," I plead. I thought loving Shea from afar was hard. Loving her and losing her, right in front of me, is so much worse.

"You take your time. But you can't expect me to wait for you. You're afraid. I don't know what you're afraid of, but whatever it is, you're going to need to face that. I would have helped if you'd let me." She shakes her head, dropping her hand. "I know that I want to be with you. I've been telling you that for two months. And I love you. I'm not sure what more there is."

She turns and heads inside, leaving me on the patio in the dark, alone.

Shea

AFTER EVERYONE LEAVES, MY mother and I clean the kitchen together in silence.

"Would you please explain to me what exactly happened to our evening?" she finally asks. "Because one moment, we were all having a lovely dinner, and the next, the Reynolds and Petersons were leaving in a rush." She cocks her head. "And Justin was holding a bag of frozen peas on his groin." She shakes her head as if trying to make sense of that one.

"Linc and I are together. Or we were until tonight, I guess." I reach for the turkey platter and a Tupperware container to hold the leftovers. "No one knew about it, but Colt found out. And he punched Linc in the face."

Next to me, my mother goes completely still. I can almost hear her processing that information and lining it up against what happened here today. "Oh boy."

"You could say that." I snap the lid on the turkey and slide it into the refrigerator.

My mom leans against the sink, one hand pressed against her temple. "And Justin..."

"I kneed him in the balls. He was trying to kiss me."

She rolls her eyes. "Oh no."

"Yep," I say, letting the *P* at the end snap.

My mother shakes her head, exhaling. "His mother has been telling me how much he misses you and how much he's wanted to talk to you. I figured that if you sat next to each other, you could explain to him kindly that things weren't meant to be."

"Well, it would be nice if you had clued me in on that."

"I didn't know about the rest of the dynamic." She frowns at me and continues. "And Linc was at the other end of the table." She drops her perfectly manicured hands into the sudsy water then vigorously scrubs at a pot. My mother usually hires servers and housekeeping for these occasions, but she sees Thanksgiving as a family affair, which apparently means that the family does the dishes. "I assume he didn't appreciate that much."

"No, he did not."

"Men can be possessive."

"Men can be idiots," I correct because between Linc and Colt, I'm pretty fed up.

My mom laughs. "Maybe." We continue to clean up in companionable silence. When we're finished, she motions to the huge island and pats the counter, reaching for two coffee mugs. "Why don't we have some of that coffee that no one got to drink?"

Nodding, I flop down on one of the barstools there. "This is a huge mess."

She places coffee in front of both of us. Then she joins me, getting on her stool with more grace than someone should manage, and pats my hand. "Well, then I suppose it's a good thing that I raised you to fix messes."

I stare at her and realize that she's right. My mom is a genius at threading the needle in hard conversations with complicated people. I used to be fascinated, watching her in social situations because I'm not naturally outgoing. It all came easily to my mother, though. She's still happily married to my father, and he's admittedly one of the strongest personalities I've ever met.

"But," she offers, "this seems to be only half your mess." She tilts her head to the side. "A third, possibly. Or something between a third and a half. You'd have to ask your father. He's the one who likes math."

"I should never have agreed to keep things a secret with Linc." I close my eyes, shaking my head.

"Why did you do that, baby?"

"Because he wanted to." I shrug helplessly. "And I wanted him."

"I can respect that. Sometimes, you have to balance what you want with what you can live with." She stands, rinses her coffee mug, and puts it in the dishwasher. "But you should definitely talk to your brother. You'll both feel better."

"I will, Mom. Give me a couple of days to get over him punching the guy I was seeing."

"Was seeing?" She lifts her brows.

"I'm still sorting it out." I have no idea what Linc and I are right now.

She gives me a hug then heads upstairs. I'm left alone to consider her words. *Balance what you want with what you can live with.*

I sit there for long moments before rinsing my mug and putting it away.

It's time I did something I should have done weeks ago. Months, maybe.

I pad on my bare feet to my father's office, carrying my heels. I knock on his door. "Dad? You up?" I hear him call from inside, so I push the door open. He's seated at his desk, his computer on and a glass of bourbon in his hand.

"Shea. I didn't expect you." He takes off the pair of glasses he started needing about five years ago and sets them on the desk.

"I know." My dad doesn't sleep much, and nighttime is when he claims to do his best thinking. It's an unspoken rule that we leave him to it rather than try to engage him when his mind is working a hundred miles an hour. "I really need to talk to you about something."

"Is it about all the gentlemen vying for your affections?" He raises his eyebrows. "Because that's probably more your mother's arena than mine."

I grin. "Dad, no one says 'vying for your affections' anymore."

"I did." He touches his forehead. "So obviously, someone's saying it."

"Right." I step farther into the office, the smile leaving my face. "Is it okay if I sit?"

He motions me into the seat across from him. I sit down, setting my shoes on the ground next to me, and take a steadying breath. "I don't want to come to work at Carmichael Enterprises next year."

My father goes from relaxed to alert in a moment. "What?"

"I know that we've always discussed me working for the design department. But I don't want to do that." I inhale. "I don't enjoy corporate design. I'd like to do residential work."

His brows drop. "No money in residential work, Shea." It's not an opinion. It's a statement.

"There's enough money to make a living, but not money like you make, no." I agree.

He opens his arms wide. "You could eventually take a leadership role at Carmichael. It's your legacy."

"I realize that. Maybe I will want to someday. But I don't want to do that right now." Leaving that door open seems to pacify him, and as I say the words, I realize they're true. I might want to do that someday. I'm proud of what my father has built.

"What do you want to do now, then?" Something I love about my father is that he gets right to the point.

My heart races. "Jackie Toulesse, my summer internship boss, would like me to work with her."

"Doing?" He purses his lips.

"Well, I'd like to talk with you about that." I take a calming breath. "And I could use your advice." This is already going much differently than I expected. "She's offered to have me open a new office for her in Brooklyn. I would give her a capital investment for a thirty percent share in her company."

My father leans back in his chair, touching his fingers together. "A capital investment."

"Yes. She would like a quarter of a million dollars."

"I bet she would." He seems to find this amusing. "And this is what you want to do? You want to work for a woman's renovation company, rehabilitating homes for rich people in Brooklyn?"

I wince and consider what he's saying. As I meet his forthright gaze, I decide something I've been struggling with for a while. "No. I don't think I do."

He raises his brows again. I get the feeling I'm surprising my father tonight. I'm surprising myself, I suppose. I rub my hands against my pants, trying to dry my sweaty palms. "I liked working for Jackie. I like renovations and rehabilitating buildings. But I don't want to only do it for rich people." I square my shoulders. "At school, I've done a couple of projects for Habitat for Humanity."

"And you've enjoyed that?" He taps the tips of his fingers together.

"I have." I nod emphatically. "In fact, it's the most fulfilling work I've ever done."

"I see." He stares over my head. I can see him calculating, already juggling possibilities in his head. The way he thinks has always fascinated me.

"What do you see? Because I can't see anything these days." I lean back in my chair. "We've always talked about me coming to Carmichael in the corporate design department. I'd work there, and Justin would be at NYU for law, and eventually, we'd get married and live happily ever after or something." I snort.

"I never really saw how that would work for you." He wrinkles his nose in distaste. "You're not the wait-around-for-a-happily-ever-after sort. You do things, honey, and you fix things. I could have told you that."

"I wish you *would* have told me that," I fire back.

He shrugs. "Not my circus."

He's right. "Since the summer, I've felt like I was on the wrong path with this."

"Why didn't you tell me? I'm a good sounding board."

He is. "I was sure you'd be upset."

"I mean, I'm a little upset you didn't say anything, but I understand." He grimaces. "I remember being twenty-one."

"I'm sorry," I offer, and I am. He is my father. I should have had a conversation with him the second I was uncertain. Isn't this what I was trying to tell Linc earlier? Have I really been any better? That makes me squirm in my seat.

Not one for emotional displays, he waves me off. "Okay, enough now. Let's talk about this investment opportunity. I was looking over a merger my legal department sent me last night, but this is much more fun."

I shake my head at him. Only my dad could say something like that. "Let me go and get the paperwork out of my room, so we can go over it." I pick up my shoes and head toward the door, stopping before I leave. "And Dad?"

"Yeah?"

"Thanks."

He sniffs. "Hurry up, now. It's getting late, and you're about to get me at my best. No time to waste."

I grin and hurry upstairs to my room to retrieve my paperwork.

Linc

AFTER WE LEAVE THE Carmichaels', I go for a drive, heading toward Montauk. I need to clear my head. I stop at a 7-Eleven for a Slurpee and press it against my lip instead of drinking it—Colt can really throw a punch. It's still throbbing when I get to the end of Long Island, and I get out to stare at the ocean in the moonlight.

I don't think I could have made a bigger mess if I'd tried.

I stand next to the fence overlooking the shoreline. Leaning on the plank, I let the raw wood dig into my palms.

Shea said I'm afraid. Of her? No, not of her. She's one of the things in the world that I do trust. But I've lost control, and that's terrifying to me. Everything is shifting under me, and I can't seem to get my footing anymore.

I push away from the fence and get back in the car. I drive home, the music up, but nothing drowns out the sound of her voice telling me that it's not her that's keeping us apart. But that only leaves me, and I don't know what to do with that.

At home, the lights are out. I glance at the dashboard clock. It's late.

I kill the engine and open the back door as softly as I can. My father's sitting at the peninsula in the kitchen. The only light on is the one over the stove. He's got two glasses in front of him, and a bottle of whiskey is open next to him. It looks like he's only been sipping, though, because it's mostly full.

I've never seen my father drink whiskey. We have it in the house for mixed drinks and punches my mom makes. Seeing him here, obviously waiting for me, is exactly not what I want tonight. "Dad, I need to get up early."

"Sit down, Linc."

I do as he asks. He pours a finger's worth of whiskey into one of my mom's stemless wine glasses and pushes it across the counter to me. I take a sip. "Thanks."

"Trying to piece together why you were bleeding at Thanksgiving dinner and why your mother insisted we leave before I got to have any of her pie."

I have another gulp, bigger than the last one. "Got punched in the face, Dad."

"I see that." He swirls the contents of his glass. "By whom? That's the real question."

I tilt my head and frown.

"Well, seems to me it could have been three different people. Colt could have punched you for being a bad friend. Shea might have hit you because you're a bad boyfriend."

Of course, my mother told my father about Shea and me. I shake my head.

"And that fancypants Peterson guy? Well, I just don't like the look of him."

"No way Peterson gets the jump on me." I doubt that dickhead knows how to throw a punch, anyway.

Dad nods. "Figured as much. That leaves the more important two."

I sigh. "Yeah."

"Well, want to clue me in? Your mom thinks it was Colt, but I've got money riding on Shea."

"It wasn't Shea." I swallow another mouthful of whiskey, appreciating the burn. "Colt."

He harrumphs. "Bleeding too much for it to have been Shea, I guess."

I blow out a breath, shaking my head. "I screwed this all up."

"Seems like that." He sips again.

"She's Colt's sister. I should have kept my hands to myself."

"Probably."

"I should have told him too."

"Definitely," he adds.

I exhale, drinking again. Dad's right. This conversation definitely needed alcohol. I drop my head into my hands. "It was going to change everything. I didn't want to change anything else." I let my hands drop on the counter. "The concussions last season and then my stupid scholarship money. My agent isn't calling me back, so I'm not sure if I'm going to be able to pull anything together for my hockey career." I gaze around at the kitchen. "Then Mom and her treatment. Avery has told me how much it costs. I feel like so many things are falling apart already."

"And you thought this was the best way to go? Lying to your best friend and keeping your relationship a secret?" My father shakes his head at me. "Listen, shit changes. There's nothing you can do about it."

"But not like this. If things were changing for the better, for the easier, that would be different."

"You want to wait for the perfect time to get going on your life?" He snorts out a laugh. "Good luck with that."

"Not perfect. Just... more figured out."

"If you wait for things to get figured out, you'll be waiting forever." He shakes his head. "You're going to need to roll with the punches." He pauses. "No pun intended."

"But it's not only me. It's you guys. It's Shea."

"Us?" He sets his glass down hard. "What are you talking about?"

"Money, Dad. We need money."

"Everyone always needs money."

"No, Dad. We really need money." Why am I explaining this to him?

"First of all," he says, scowling at me, "I know what we need. I'm the father around here. And that was why I took out a loan, Linc. On the house."

"You did what?"

"We have equity. The housing market is on a rise, so I cashed in some. Your mom's treatment and your school are what is important right now." He shrugs. "We'll figure it out later."

I can only blink at him.

"And Shea? I bet that she doesn't expect you to have it all figured out either. Things are going to go right, and things are going to go wrong. That doesn't mean you stop." He sighs and drains his glass. "Those concussions messed with your head, kid, and not just physically." He claps me on the shoulder, puts his glass in the sink, and leaves me in the dark with my thoughts.

Linc

WE LOSE BOTH OF our Thanksgiving weekend hockey matchups. I don't know whether the opponents are that good, or if we just are off our game. Declan's playing like shit—every one of his impulsive behaviors is on display on the ice. Ash isn't helping him out. His head seems to be all over the place. I have no idea what happened during their holiday. I can only assume it was as bad as mine.

It's almost finals, too, so everyone's on edge. Thursday, after my ten o'clock class, I get a voicemail from my agent. I've been trying to get ahold of him for weeks, so I dial him right back, hoping that he's free.

Thank God, he picks up. "Linc. How are you?"

"Good, Howie. I'm sorry, but I haven't even listened to your voicemail. I wanted to call you right back. I'm hoping you have good news for me."

"I wish I did, Linc." He sighs, and the weight of it carries over the line and into my stomach. "But the Gladiators have decided that they'd like to wait until further into your season to make a decision about your contract."

I exhale slowly, trying to blow out the anxiety that's bottled into my chest. "Damn."

"They're watching you very closely, buddy. But they need more time to make decisions after your concussions. And now that you're out with your groin, they've decided to wait until closer to playoffs."

"That makes perfect sense. It really does." It's rational, but it doesn't help me.

"I'll be back in touch with you after the new year. We'll talk more then, okay?"

"Sounds good. Thanks for calling me back," I say then disconnect.

I pocket my phone. Everyone is hurrying to their classes around me, but all I can do is stand with my hands in my hair. My heart races in my chest, and I do my best to breathe through the panic inside me.

Why am I freaking out? This isn't a no. It's a wait-and-see. A racing heart and sweaty palms aren't a rational response.

A text message dings through on my phone from Declan*: Our team will be helping this weekend at a Habitat for Humanity project here in town. We only have one game on Friday night, so plan to spend Saturday and Sunday getting your hands dirty.*

I reread the message twice. That's Shea's project. She must have asked Declan to message the team instead of me.

Because she doesn't want to talk to me.

I glance around, my eyes unfocused. No one seems to notice that my world is a complete disaster. They're going about their lives, oblivious.

I go to my next class. As I listen to the professor go over the details for a final paper due next week, I decide exactly what I need to sort through this.

My best friend.

When the professor dismisses us, I pull my phone out of my pocket and pull up the message thread from Colt. I stand in the hallway outside my class and think about what I need to say. There are so many things I've done wrong, so many things we've left unspoken. It all ends with one sentiment, though.

Me: *I'm sorry I lied to you.*

Two hours later, I'm in Philadelphia. The drive gives me time to clear my head. It also lets me plan what I'm going to say to my best friend, who punched me in the face a week ago.

He lives in Old City in Philadelphia. He shares his place with another young guy on the Tyrants team, Rocco Barnett. It's close to all the downtown bars and restaurants, where a lot of the nightlife in the city happens. Not too bad for a twenty-one-year-old guy.

I park a few blocks away, and he's sitting on the front steps as I walk up. "Hey."

He appears to brace himself. "Hey."

I sit next to him. It's chilly, so the concrete stairs are cold. The sounds of the city around us are the only things that fill the silence for long minutes.

"I should have told you." I clasp my hands together, my elbows on my knees. "I'm really sorry. I wanted to tell you."

"Why didn't you, then?" Colt asks. I can tell he's trying to remain calm, but calm's never been his forte. "We text almost every day. There had to have been a time when it could have come up."

"You think this is something I could tell you over text?" I laugh incredulously. "'Good luck on your game tonight. By the way, I'm in love with your sister.'"

"I just don't get how this happened." His eyes widen. "When? How? What happened?"

"When? I guess... always?" I shrug. "But you are my best friend. I did what I could to fight it. I figured it was teenage crush stuff, and I wasn't about to screw things up with you. I knew how you felt about the guys on the team and Shea."

"Yeah, there's them, and then there's you."

"I should have been better than them. I tried to be better than them."

He buries his hands in his hair.

"You went to juniors, and she started dating Peterson. She seemed happy with him. She spent a lot of the last three years at State with him. I'd see her when she was on campus, but I kept my distance. I told myself that whatever I felt for her was a leftover childhood crush and sisterly affection." I shake my head. "I'm an idiot."

"Sometimes, yeah. You are."

I chuckle. "When she broke up with him, I started to see her more. It became impossible to ignore how I felt. But we didn't get together until New York, after the gala."

"It's been almost two months, then." He looks at me, eyes narrowed. "You and Shea kept this a secret for two months."

"She wanted to tell you. She wanted to tell you from the beginning. I convinced her to wait." I need him to know that the responsibility lies with me.

"Why the fuck would you do that?" He scowls at me. "Fine, I'd have been upset at first. I might still have punched you."

I snort out a laugh. "Fine."

"But I would have gotten over it. Jesus, Linc. I want to see you both happy."

"It's not only that I thought you'd be upset, though." I exhale because this is the harder part for me. "The rest of my fucking life is a hot-ass mess."

"What do you mean?"

"My mom... she's having chemotherapy to try to stem her MS flare-ups. My father says that the doctors are optimistic, but it's really expensive, like, we-can't-pay-for-it expensive. Plus, the concussions made me lose my room-and-board allowance this year. We've had to pay for all of that out of pocket." I open my hands and take a breath. "And I've been having panic attacks."

"What?" His mouth drops open. "For how long?"

"Since the doctors cleared me to skate. I couldn't make myself get out on the ice all summer. I'd get to the rink, even lace up, then wimp out like a fucking pussy."

"Jesus Christ." His eyes are wide. "Why didn't you say something?"

"Because if I said something, more people would know. And the more people that knew, the more real it was. I figured if I could push through. If I could get on the ice, it would be fine. Then no one would have to worry. And if I got on the ice, I could get back up to tiptop shape, and then the Gladiators would finally sign me. If the Gladiators sign me, then I get paid."

"That's a whole lot of 'ifs,' buddy." He sounds sympathetic.

"Yeah."

"What does any of that have to do with you and Shea, though?"

"What kind of a boyfriend can I be to your sister, literally the best person I know, when I'm all fucking tangled up in my head?" I rub my jaw. "I kept thinking that if things turned around—things with the team, my contract, my mom, something—that I wouldn't feel quite so much like I was dragging a bunch of baggage to her door. Then I could be the boyfriend she deserves."

"You're my best friend, but you're acting like an idiot."

I exhale. "Jesus, Colt—"

"First of all, why the fuck haven't you said anything about this?"

"It's a lot—"

"And I'm your friend. That's what friends do. We tell each other shitty stuff that's happening to us."

"You never tell me shitty stuff," I point out.

"Yes, I do." He punches me in the leg. "I've literally been bugging you since the spring about Shea. How worried I was about her."

"Well, yeah, but that's because I care about her too."

"I know." His expression tells me that was obvious. "And don't you think that Shea and I have been talking about you?"

"What do you mean?"

"You've been weird. You weren't around all summer. You've been distant. We're worrying about you, too, you asshole."

"Why didn't you say anything?"

"Because you're supposed to tell us if something's wrong." He shakes his head. "Holy shit, you're dense. I ask about your mom. I ask about hockey. You're supposed to fill in the blanks, dumbass."

I laugh. "Well, that's not how things work in my family. We make jokes, pretend nothing is wrong, and hope shit just goes away."

"Extremely healthy."

I give him the finger, and he laughs.

We sit in companionable silence for long minutes. Finally, he asks, "Have you spoken with Shea?"

I shake my head. "I've texted her. She won't write me back."

"Me neither." He shrugs. "She didn't like that I punched you."

"I didn't like that part much either."

"So, what are you going to do?" he asks. When I look at him, he drops his eyebrows and his mouth thins. "How are you going to fix things with her?"

"I have no fucking clue."

"Well, you need to figure something out, pal. Because you can date my sister, but if you treat her like shit, I'm going to hit you again."

I hold my hands up. "Fair enough."

"Come on." He stands, holding his hand out to me. "Let's go get a drink. We can try to figure out how to fix things with Shea."

I take his hand, and he hikes me up.

"And about the rest of it? If you need anything, ask, okay?"

I nod, swallowing the lump in my throat. For the first time in a while, I don't feel the anxiety clawing at my chest.

Shea

MY HABITAT FOR HUMANITY project is scheduled for the weekend after finals are over. Without the distraction of final exams, though, I spend most of Friday thinking about Linc.

I don't go to the game on Friday night. Instead, I stay home and watch six episodes of the newest romcom on Netflix, drink most of a bottle of wine, and eat a pint of Ben & Jerry's.

There must be healthier ways to manage breakups.

The first week after Thanksgiving, I did okay. But as the days went by, I started to doubt myself.

Is this really what I'm supposed to do when someone I love is hurting—leave them to their own devices? Then I remember all the times I asked him to talk to me. I gave him a million opportunities to let me in. That's when I get angry.

When I'm not mad or plagued with doubt, I'm sad and lonely. I haven't been good company the past two weeks.

I saw him on my way to class one morning. He looked haunted. I spent the entire class trying to decide whether I should text him or not. He's left at least a dozen messages for me.

Colt sends me a few messages too, but I'm not ready to make nice with him yet. This isn't entirely his fault, but he could have taken things better than he did if he'd focused more on being my brother and less on having hurt feelings.

He certainly didn't need to punch anyone.

Mostly, I've been moping around and trying not to mope around for two weeks. It's exhausting.

Saturday morning of my project is slower than it needs to be, thanks to the Friday night wine. I throw my hair in a messy ponytail, grab a Gatorade out of my refrigerator, and head over. I'm thankful I'm only half an hour behind.

The hockey team is already here.

I debated calling them in. Linc said that the team thought the last project was a good bonding experience, though, and I can't pretend we don't need their help. I've gotten to know this Habitat family even better over the past month while designing their house, and if anyone deserves to get going on their new start as soon as possible, it's them.

With enough help, we should have them in their new home by Christmas.

As I head up the walkway to the house, though, there are more big and bulky guys here than I expected. I pause, studying them closer, until I realize that it's not only the Chesterboro team working on the house. There are players I recognize from my brother's team, the Philadelphia Tyrants, here as well.

I hurry up the stairs. Griffin's standing on the porch, drinking from a water bottle. "Hey, Shea. We were wondering when you'd get here."

I smooth my hand over my hair. "I had a hard time getting up." I glance around. "What's going on?" The place is teeming with hockey players. Inside, Kyla, the project coordinator, looks like she's in shock.

"You should give Linc another shot, Pint Size. He's sorry he screwed up."

"What?" I ask. But Griff's headed down the stairs already. "Griff?" I call, but he ignores me, disappearing out of sight. I can only step inside.

Kyla sees me and hurries over. "Shea. How did you do this?" I shake my head. "It's the Bulldog team and the Philadelphia Tyrants." She waves around us, where people are working in pretty much every corner of the place. "Then some of the other volunteers sent messages to their friends, telling them it's a hockey-player bonanza in here, and now, we have even more people coming soon."

I press my hand to my forehead, completely speechless.

She stands in front of me, squeezing my forearms. "We might be able to finish this weekend." She hugs me happily.

"That's"—I search for the right word— "that's wonderful. Truly." I glance around the room. "Is my brother here?" I haven't talked to Colt since Thanksgiving. To see him here, where I don't expect him, is a surprise.

She nods. It doesn't even strike me as strange that she knows exactly who my brother is. "He's in the kitchen."

I nod and step through the door. What I find stops me in my tracks.

My brother is removing the cabinets. He's covered in sweat, swinging a sledgehammer. It's a construction site, so that's not that strange. What sucks the air out of my lungs is that Linc is standing nearby, holding a set of blueprints, bossing him around.

"It says here that that soffit, above the cabinets, has to come down. They want to put cabinets clear up to the ceiling."

My brother scowls over his shoulder at him. "That's easy for you to say. You don't have to do any of the hard work because of your silly groin pull."

"My groin is very serious."

Colt rolls his eyes and grunts, swinging the hammer again. That's when he catches sight of me. His smile becomes wider. "Hey, Tiny. You're late."

I find my voice. "Why are you here?" Colt and Linc exchange a glance. "And why are you two talking? You punched him in the face two weeks ago."

Colt shrugs. "We're over it."

"Well, good for you." I glare at them both, but when Linc's eyes meet mine, it's hard to keep a fierce face. He stands, tucks his hands into his pockets, and walks toward me.

Why does he have to look like this? His hair's longer, curling around his ears. There are still bags under his eyes, like he's exhausted, but the look he's giving me is so tentative and beautiful, it takes my breath away. His lips tilt up, and that dimple... "Hi."

I can't be here. I turn and push out the back door. Except the backyard is full of people, too, so I keep going, heading around the side of the house, desperate to find some solitude so I can get my thoughts together.

"Shea," he calls from behind me. "Please, wait..."

He catches my hand, and I stop. He rubs his thumb against the inside of my wrist, and tingles rush through me.

How can he do that with one touch? "Linc." I inhale, trying to hold on to the frayed strands of my thoughts. "I'm glad you and Colt made up, but..."

"This isn't about Colt and me, Shea." He takes my other hand, now, holding both in his. "It's about you and me."

I exhale. “Linc...” I don’t know what he’s about to say, but I brace myself. I’m not sure I can live through another explanation about what’s wrong with us and why things can’t work.

“Please, hear me out.” He squeezes my fingers. Then he shakes my hands, blowing out an unsteady breath. “God, this is harder than I thought. I’m so fucking happy to see you and touch you.” He shakes his head. “Okay, here goes. I’m sorry. So sorry. I should have done so many things differently. I should have told you and Colt about how bad things were a long time ago.” He blows the hair out of his eyes. “It’s hard for me. Talking about stuff like that... it doesn’t come easy to me. But I promise that I’ll do better. You might need to prod me sometimes, but I swear, I’ll do my best from now on.

“But more importantly, I should have told you how I felt about you.” He steps closer and raises a hand, reaching for my face slowly, as if he isn’t sure I’m going to allow his touch.

I close my eyes, tilting my cheek into his palm.

He smooths my hair off my forehead. “When you were dating Justin, I thought you were happy, that you were where you belonged. But when you broke up with him, I didn’t want anyone else to make you happy. I wanted to be the one for you. God, you asked me to help you find someone new.” He chuckles. “I’m surprised I didn’t lose my mind, thinking about you with anyone else.”

I duck my head, the weight of this new hope is almost too heavy.

“You’ve always been it for me, Shea, and if I wasn’t so twisted up in my own fucking head, I would never have let you think anything else.” He drops light kisses all over my face. “I love you so much. Please, be my girlfriend. Be my everything. I want to tell everyone. I want to be with you always. I want to tell you everything that happens to me." He grimaces. "Even the shit that sucks. Just please say you'll go through all that with me, because nothing has been as hard as the past two weeks without you."

I meet his gaze again, and I can see the sincerity in his eyes. "Yes. Yes, please."

He drops his mouth to mine, claiming me hungrily and intensely. I stand on tiptoes in my sneakers and dig my fingers through his messy hair, pulling him closer. I curl my body into him as he leans over me. His fingers press into my back, and I lose track of how many kisses we share.

Finally, he pulls away. "We need to get out of here." He snags my hand in his and starts hauling me toward the front of the house. Around us, the sounds of the construction site continue, but when we round the corner to the front yard, I hear wolf whistles. Searching for the source of them, I find Declan and Griff on the porch clapping as Ash whistles, his fingers between his teeth. "Way to go, Shea! Way to go, Linc!"

Linc holds up our joined hands, like the victor in a boxing match. "I love her!" he yells up to them.

"We know!" Declan calls down.

When others in the yard start to turn toward us, Linc opens his arms wide. "Did you all hear?" he shouts. "I love Shea Carmichael!"

"Shut up, you idiot," I mumble, but I don't really mean it. I feel the color high on my cheeks.

Now, though, everyone's getting into the celebration. There are catcalls and whoops all over the job site, and Linc sweeps me into his arms, dropping a kiss on my lips right there in front of everyone. When we pull away, I'm breathless and laughing helplessly.

My brother's standing on the front steps, watching us. He winks at me then points two fingers to his eyes, and then at Linc, the universal I'm-watching-you sign. Linc salutes him then hurries me down the street to his car.

"Where are we going?" I gasp, tripping along behind him.

"To my place. Or yours. Or to a quiet spot somewhere so I can kiss every inch of you."

"We can't just leave." I motion back to where everyone's still clapping. "They need us."

"I need you." He spins me around, gathering me close again. "Right now, Shea. We'll come back. I swear."

Staring into his eyes, I don't care what anyone else thinks—not my brother, not the entire hockey team, not even an entire professional hockey team. "Yes. Let's go."

Linc

WE GO TO SHEA'S place because it's closer than mine. The semester is over, so there aren't many people around. We hurry up the stairs and down the hall, and then she's fumbling with the key to get in.

As soon as the door is open, I sweep her up into my arms and hustle us right into the bedroom. I have her on the bed before the door even clicks closed behind us.

We struggle out of our clothes. Between rushing and trying to keep kissing in between, we're clumsy about it. I fumble with the button on her pants as she tugs my sweatshirt over my head. But after long moments, we're finally naked together.

I pause, closing my eyes, reveling in the feel of her skin against mine. How, in any demented recess of my mind, did I think that anything was worth giving her up? The past weeks without her have been infinitely harder. I still had all the bullshit—injury, sick mom, money issues—but without her, I couldn't even think properly.

"I love you," I say as I open my eyes. "I'm so sorry I pushed you away. I'll never do that again."

She sweeps my hair off my face, smiling up at me. "You'll probably try. But I'm not going to let you." She tugs my head down to hers, and I kiss her. It's like coming back home.

I make true on my promise. I kiss every inch of her that I can get my mouth on, starting with her face and neck and down her chest. I suck on her nipples and run my fingers down the length of her arms and legs, exploring all her warm and soft places. By the time I cover myself with a condom, her eyes are glazed over, her hair is strewn around her on the bed, and I can barely breathe from how beautiful she is to me.

I cup her cheek with my hand as I push into her body. "I love you."

She arches, moaning out my name. "I love you too."

We move, clinging to one another. This time with her is different than the others. This time, I feel like she sees inside me. That's probably because I've let her see, and knowing that she does—that she's seen my ugliest and she still finds it in her to love me anyway—well, that touches something deep inside me.

It makes me feel for the first time in a long time that everything might really be okay.

Our movements become more frantic, and when we come, me right after her, I'm left with only the deepest sense of contentment.

I pull her against me, dropping my face into the curve where her neck meets her shoulder, and breathe her in. She wiggles her backside against me and damned if my dick doesn't stir again.

She tilts her head as I lick her neck, sighing. "We absolutely cannot do that again right now."

"Why not?"

She squirms out of my grasp and sits up. Her hair is wild around her face. Her lips are pink, and the color's high on her face. She's lovely.

She is my girl. I grin at her, propping my head up on my elbow.

"What are you smiling about?" she teases me.

"You're just always so put together. Gorgeous, all the time. But I like you best this way." I shrug.

She blushes. "Come on, lazy. They're waiting for us back at the job."

"All right, all right," I grumble, but there's no heat to it. Right now, I don't think anything could bother me.

I reach for my clothes where we chucked them around her room. That's when I see a bunch of applications strewn on the nightstand. "What's this?" I ask.

"Oh." Her face lights up. "I'm applying to graduate school."

"What? No way. When did you decide this?" I hate that I missed her deciding something like this.

"Thanksgiving, actually." She sits down in her pants and her bra, picking up the top two packets. "This is Columbia, and this is NYU. I'm only applying to the schools in New York." She grins at me shyly. "Though if you'd like, I can look at Boston too."

"Wait, stop. Start at the beginning."

"I told you about Jackie's offer." She lifts her eyebrows, and I nod.

"Of course. She wanted you to open a branch of her company in Brooklyn." We'd talked about it on the way back to school, the day she got the job offer.

"Yes."

"But you didn't know if you wanted it."

"I didn't. I don't." She shakes her head. "I finally got up the nerve to talk to my dad on Thanksgiving. After our fight." She glances down, and I squeeze her hand. "Well, after that, I realized that I told you that you should talk to the people you care about when things were bothering you. But I wasn't taking my own advice. I was avoiding telling my father about my concerns about working for him. So I did. And I realized that he was the perfect one to talk out Jackie's offer with." She shrugs. "He's Rory Carmichael, one of the top ten biggest real estate moguls in the world."

"Does sound like a good option for business advice."

She laughs. "Well, I spilled my guts about how I didn't want to work in corporate design. How Jackie wanted him to invest in her company in exchange for her giving me a plum job."

"That wasn't exactly how you explained it to me..." I scowl. "She recognizes your talent."

"And she recognizes that my father is rich." She smiles knowingly. "I'm not naïve, Linc." She waves at the applications. "But I also told Dad how much I loved Habitat for Humanity and working on renovations, especially when they helped a community."

"Okay..."

"He suggested that I could do more good if I went to work for him at Carmichael to oversee their corporate investment into local gentrification programs." She wrinkles her nose. "I think he also liked the idea that I'd be working at Carmichael. It's my father, after all. He likes to get what he wants."

"So..." I draw her back to the story.

"So... I'd love to do something like that. Carmichael is flush with money, and the company has the resources to do a lot of good, investing in communities." She bites into her lip. "But I told him that I didn't know enough about the cultural, economic, and government policy involved in gentrification. It seems like there's a fine line between investing money into a place to improve it and improving it so much that the people who would benefit the most are priced out."

She picks up the application. "I decided to look into master's programs that focused on urban planning and community development. If I'm going to helm something like this, I need to be as educated about it as possible so I can bring in educated people and make decisions that truly bring change to neighborhoods that need it."

I scoop her into a hug. "That's probably the greatest thing I've ever heard. It's the perfect fit for you. You can design, you can make old things new again, and you can help people."

She laughs as I kiss her on the cheek. "I hope so. But I'm a bit late getting my applications in..." She worries her bottom lip with her teeth.

"You'll get it done. You can do anything you put your mind to."

"But..." She scowls up at me, poking me in the middle of my chest. "That means that I need to get back to that job site. I'll need Kyla's recommendation. I doubt this is the best way to get it. Running off to have sex with my boyfriend in the middle of a project..."

I rub the spot where she poked me. "Ouch. Between you and your brother, always hurting me."

She rolls her eyes, throwing her Habitat for Humanity shirt back on.

When she's done, I pull her back into my arms for another quick hug. "I'm so happy for you. I can't wait to see the things you do."

"Thanks." She grins. "Now, come on. You need to boss my brother around some more. He deserves it. I'm still annoyed that he hit you."

"Cut him some slack." I slide into my sweatshirt. "He's made up for it since."

"He did?"

"Yeah." We leave, pulling the door closed behind us. Since I visited him in Philadelphia, I've tried to be better about answering questions honestly. I'm still not good at it sometimes. My first instinct is to deflect, deny, and play things off with a joke. It'll take a long time to relearn old habits. But I'm trying.

"Huh," Shea says, studying me as we walk down the stairs. "Well, that's good, then."

I nod. As we head back to where I parked my car, I agree. Things are good. For the first time in a long time, I think maybe everything might actually be okay.

Shea

IT'S THE WEEKEND BEFORE Christmas, and we're at my parents' penthouse on the Upper East Side for their holiday party. It's always a fancy affair, so I let my mom pick something out for me to wear, a velvet sheath that falls to an A-line at mid-calf, which I paired with the most sparkly pair of gold heels I could find.

Linc is breathtakingly handsome in his tuxedo. In the past two weeks, he's been more open with his thoughts and feelings, and it seems to have helped some. I'm not sure whether that's what's helping him sleep at night or whether it's because we're in each other's beds, but whatever it is, he looks healthier and happier than he has in a while.

He still has a lot going on, but he's doing what he can to let go of things he can't control. Luckily, Mrs. Reynolds has improved a lot since her first chemo treatment. The medicine is hard on her, but it seems to be doing what they hoped it would. She hasn't had any flare-ups since her first dose, and she's more energetic than she's been in a long time. Also, because his father took out their second mortgage, there's not as much immediate threat of financial issues, though Linc is obviously still hoping things work out with the Gladiators by season's end.

I'm happy because his groin is officially healed, and he's ready to get back on the ice, two weeks earlier than expected. Right now, it doesn't appear to bother him at all as he waltzes me around the dance floor.

Tonight, I'm celebrating the fact that I managed to get all my graduate school applications in—including references—and I only had to pay for one late fee. The applications include one to Boston College and one to Boston University, just in case.

"Want to take a break?" he asks as the song comes to an end, and a waltz starts.

Across the room, I make eye contact with Justin. He glances away quickly, probably remembering my knee to his crotch at the last holiday get-together. I expect to feel some emotion—sadness, nostalgia, anger, anything—but I don't. I can't, not with Linc here with me.

He's what I want, and I'm not afraid to be happy with him.

I crook a finger at him, and he leans down to kiss me. "What was that for?" he asks softly against my mouth.

I can only grin at him. "When you get what you want, it's important to never forget how lucky you are."

He traces the curve of my cheek. "I love you."

"I love you too," I say. "One more dance?" Since our first waltz, I've been unable to resist the chance to slide around the dance floor with him.

"Anytime, anywhere."

"Don't let me fall?" I tease as he takes me into his arms.

"I'll carry you anywhere, tiny girl."

I pull him down and kiss him again before as he sweeps me up and across the dance floor.

About the Author

Josie Blake writes college-set, hockey romance with sass and emotion. She also writes award-winning romantic suspense and scifi thrillers as Marnee Blake. You can find out more about that here.

Originally from a small town in western Pennsylvania, she now battles traffic in southern New Jersey where she lives with her hero husband and their happily-ever-after: two very energetic sons. When she isn't writing, she can be found next to a hockey rink or swimming pool, cooking up something sweet, or hiding from encroaching dust bunnies with a book.

She loves to hear from readers so please feel free to drop her a note or visit her website at josieblake.com.

Connect with her on Instagram at instagram.com/josieblakeauthor, or on Facebook at facebook.com/JosieBlakeAuthor

Made in the USA
Monee, IL
04 May 2023

33061804R00149